THE JOURNEY OF A MIRROR

THE JOURNEY OF A MIRROR

OF A MIRROR

A Woman's Endeavour & Her Quest for Love

RUNGEEN SINGH

PARTRIDGE
A Penguin Random House Company

To order additional copies of this book, contact
Partridge India
000 800 10062 62
www.partridgepublishing.com/india
orders.india@partridgepublishing.com

DEDICATED

To my lovely family specially my husband
who lovingly accepted me as I am.

For him I can truly say

'Behind every successful woman is a man
who tells her that she is absolutely right.'

CHAPTER 1

Aina! Her family had named her Aina, meaning 'a mirror'. Even at the age of fourteen she looked frail. It was as if she was fragile and could break easily like a mirror. And that was true about her. Aina was full of fears and tears as she had become very timid. This was because, her mother Gomti was callous in her attitude towards Aina, and she tried to suppress whatever spirit Aina had in her. This timidity suited those times, as, at that time, women were not supposed to have an entity of their own. They were like bonded slaves. But still, when Aina became angry, she could be bold and rebellious.

On 31st May of the year 1952, the eager Aina was standing on the terrace, where all the children of her large joint family were playing. Aina was not permitted to play with them by her mother. Generally she was not even allowed to come to the terrace, as her mother Gomti forced Aina to help in the daily household chores, even while the rest of the children played. Today her mother was busy, so Aina had sneaked up to the terrace where the boys were flying kites and the girls were playing hopscotch. Now Aina was eagerly waiting near the parapet, looking out for her dear grandfather, who was coming back to stay with them permanently.

Suddenly, without warning, her cousin Raju picked her up and bent her half over the parapet wall of the terrace, which was on the second floor of the palace.

"Ooooooh!" Aina screamed loudly and then she got paralysed with fright, as she could see the sheer drop down to the cobbled ground below, with nothing to cushion her fall. She heard Raju shout, "What if I let you fall?" and Aina nearly fainted. Aina started trembling with fright. Usually Raju was the villain in Aina's life and her young Sabal chacha (uncle) was her saviour. Seeing her agony, Sabal scolded Raju, and made him set Aina free.

Just then Aina heard the anger-infused voice of her mother. "Aina. Aina. Where are you?"

Aina spoke aloud in her frenzy, "I must go or Ma will punish me."

Raju said loudly, laughing tauntingly at her, "Yes, Aina go fast, you timid mouse, or you will be beaten again by your mother. In the morning you have already been beaten by her for waking up late."

It was true. Aina had spent a sleepless night because her grandmother had told her ghost stories before sleeping. So Aina had woken up late and her mother Gomti had thrashed Aina for it.

Aina now heard her cousins Raju, Om and Som guffaw loudly behind her back and knew that they were laughing at her. She felt humiliated and suddenly she became angry and forgot all her fears. She turned and ran back to the unsuspecting Raju and pushed him from behind. Raju fell down, and satisfied with her revenge, Aina ran down the stairs. She knew that Raju would not retaliate in front of all the women.

She quickly entered the covered inner courtyard meant for all the women. She saw her mother Gomti standing in front, looking furious; her fair, beautiful face quite marred by the ugliness of her anger.

Gomti slapped Aina and shouted, "You wretch! Where were you? I have been calling you for so long. Now sit down and peel these onions and potatoes."

Aina pleaded, "I want to go outside as Baba is coming. Please let me go outside, Ma."

Gomti replied, "Shut up. I have told you that you should obey me or you will see my dead face."

Gomti often used this ploy to make Aina obey. Aina had not taken this threat seriously at first, but then five years back, one day, she had seen all the women of her house, crying. She had asked her mother, "What is the matter? Why are you all crying?"

"Raju's mother died last night," said her Ma.

"She was not very old. Why did she die Ma?" asked Aina anxiously, because she didn't like sorrow.

"Because Raju never obeyed her, so he had to see his mother's dead face," answered Gomti.

Aina froze. She could well believe that Raju could disobey his mother. So she now trusted what Gomti had said. It sank into her brain and became an implicit belief. Yes, if a child was disobedient, then the mother could die. After that, whenever Aina felt like disobeying her mother, she would stop herself and think, "I must obey her, or she might die and I don't want her to die because of me. Oh God! Keep her alive."

As Aina picked up the knife to peel onions, she heard a carriage come inside their cobbled courtyard, which was the size of a small football field. Cries of, "He has come," rang out all over the huge palace and nearly all the male members of the family rushed down to meet their patriarch, Mahavir, to touch his feet and welcome him. Aina too got up and ran outside, before her mother Gomti could stop her. The other women could not come outside their private quarters, as they had to remain in purdah (cloister). Aina was allowed to come outside to the men's quarters, as she was still considered small.

Mahavir Chandra, (whom Aina called Baba), had come back finally to live a retired life with his huge joint family. He had retired from his service as the accountant to the Nawab of Najapur and the old Nawab had been generous enough to send Mahavir home in his personal carriage. While Mahavir was being welcomed by the men, Aina climbed into the carriage and pretended that she was a queen. She loved the rich red velvet tapestry and the tall stately white horse, but this pleasure was shortlived. She had to get down and sadly she saw the horse carriage being taken away back to the Nawab.

Aina thought, "One day I will definitely have a grand carriage like this." Then Aina ran towards Mahavir who was short and stout, with a pleasant face. His wife Parwati was short and thin with a long nose. Everyone respected the easy going Mahavir as the karta (head) of the family, but most of them were afraid of Parwati, who managed the house with an iron hand. No one could disobey her orders. All the family members gave their earnings to Parwati and she ruled unchallenged.

Mahavir and Parwati had five daughters who were all married. They had only one son Kalka who did not work at all. He was just interested in acting in plays and having a good time, drinking and going to the dancing girl Bijlee's house. Kalka was married to the fair and beautiful Gomti, who remained angry with him, as he frequented Bijlee's house. Kalka and Gomti had two children, Aina and a son Munna, whom Gomti loved and pampered. So Munna had become a spoilt boy.

Mahavir's real younger brother Prasad also lived in the palace with his wife Rukmini. They were the most mismatched couple of the family. Rukmini was fair and plump with a ready smile on her sweet face, while Prasad was without an extra ounce of flesh, as if he hated extravagance of any kind. Rukmini respected him for his high principles and he tolerated her playfulness because he knew that she had a heart of gold.

They had three children; Girish, Sabal and Prabal. Aina was afraid of her strict Prasad baba but she loved his young wife Rukmini and their son Sabal. Girish and Prabal were very reserved, but Sabal was kind.

In the palace, five cousin brothers of Mahavir and Prasad also lived with their families, but Aina was not emotionally attached to them. Those cousins often bullied her, so she tried her best to stay away from them.

CHAPTER 2

When Aina reached Mahavir, she heard his younger brother Prasad ask, "Has the final settlement of your retirement, been done by the Nawab?"

Mahavir replied, "Yes. The complete village with all its farmlands will continue to be with me. I can go on collecting their revenue as pension. The Nawab gave me ten thousand rupees cash, which is a lot of money. This palace has been given to me for a lease of ninety nine years. I am quite happy with the settlement."

"That is very good. The Nawab has been very generous. Congratulations," said his brother Prasad.

"Congratulations to you too. The Nawab praised me also," said Mahavir.

Prasad said, "You deserve it, as you have given so many years of your life in serving him so sincerely."

Kalka asked his father Mahavir, "Pitaji (father). We want to have a celebration for your coming back home. Will it be all right if I call Bijli to dance tonight?"

Mahavir knew that his son Kalka was personally interested in Bijli, still he said, "Yes, that is fine Kalka."

Then Mahavir took out a bag of money and gave it to Kalka, saying, "Now take this money which is the final settlement with the Nawab, and go and give it to your mother." Kalka took the bag of money inside.

Aina ran after him. Kalka went to the outer door of the inner courtyard and called out to his mother

Parwati, "Ma. Father has come and he is fine. The Nawab has made a very good settlement. Father has given this money for you to keep."

Parwati replied, "So his Lordship has come. Now the whole day through, he will chew my brain."

Her younger sister-in-law Rukmini said daringly, "Parwati Jijji (sister), you are actually very happy that he has come back, but you don't want to show it."

Parwati of the acerbic tongue, was tongue-tied for the first time in her life, as all the women present giggled at the teasing. Parwati conceded in her mind that it would really be nice to have her husband home every day, but she couldn't say that in front of the rest of the family. That would have been shameless!

Kalka gave the money to Aina, who went inside the courtyard and gave the money to her grandmother Parwati. Aina was used to acting as a messenger and carrier between the men and the women.

Kalka called out, "Ma. Get preparations done for a celebration. We are calling Bijli tonight."

The women in the courtyard froze. Everyone looked at Kalka's wife Gomti, who suddenly seemed to be near to tears. Aina felt alarmed to see her mother Gomti in this state.

Rukmini said, "Why is Kalka calling Bijli out of all the nautch girls? He could have called someone else."

Parwati snapped, "You mind your own business."

Suddenly Aina heard one aunt whisper, "Who is Bijli?"

The other whispered back, "Kalka is interested in this Bijli. She is his mistress."

Parwati said sharply, "Stop talking and do your work. We will need more snacks to go with the drinks in the evening, so make them quickly. Tell the servants to spray water out in the courtyard. They should also clean up the outer hall for the celebration and put mattresses on the floor and cover them with clean white sheets. Tell them to spray 'khus perfume' everywhere."

Surprisingly, none of the women felt bad that their husbands would see a dancing girl sing and dance. It was like a tradition and the women accepted it. The women of the household would also see the nautch girl perform, but they would all sit behind a curtain, so that the men couldn't see them.

Even keeping a mistress was quite acceptable and there was no stigma attached, rather it was like a high status symbol for the men.

This was because the husbands and wives had no privacy. A mating room was a separate room kept just for the 'mating' in the night, of a husband and his wife. This was the arrangement for the only sexual intimacy between couples, as the women and men of the joint family, had separate quarters in the palace.

The exploitation of women irked Prasad, the younger brother of Mahavir. He wanted to reform society and he would take out strong processions to boycott such social evils. But he felt frustrated because his own family would never listen to him.

Now Aina too, was feeling frustrated as she could not talk to her Mahavir Baba. Aina yearned to have time alone with her Baba. She wanted to tell him that her cousin Raju and some other cousins always bullied her. And she had also got to tell him how someone was stalking her. Her mother and grandmother had not believed her. Would her Baba believe her? Aina really hoped he would.

Aina loved her Baba (grandfather), Mahavir Chandra. He was very kind and partial towards her and he doted on her, but he had not lived at home all the time. Now Aina felt very happy that her Baba had come back to stay permanently and would not go away again. Aina was delighted because now she could live a better life, as her Baba would protect her from her mother.

Aina often thought, "When Baba loves me so much, I should not cry. I should follow Baba's advice to me, 'Just celebrate life and be happy'." But despite this, tears frequented her eyes as she was very vulnerable.

Now Aina looked around the palatial room while waiting for her Baba to come to his room so that she could talk to him. The palace had many big rooms with big manual fans made of bamboo and cloth tied to the ceiling, manouvred with ropes, which would be pulled by servants to cool the rooms. There were lovely, ornate chandeliers, a remnant of the glory when the Nawab's mother had lived in this palace before the Nawab had given it to Mahavir. But the rest of the palace was more tuned to utility than to beauty, because of the practical multifarious needs of the huge joint family that lived in it now. The palace was simply bursting at the seams with people, because it was normal for couples to have a lot of children. One of Mahavir's cousins in the palace had seventeen children out of whom, only ten had survived.

Then Aina saw Mahavir coming to his room. She ran to him. He held out his arms and Aina ran into them.

Mahavir said, "Oh Aina! How are you, my pet?"

"I am not all right Baba. No one believes me when I tell them my problems," said Aina.

"Don't worry. I have come now," said Mahavir.

9

"Baba, will you stay in the house always? Will you never go away from me now?' said Aina.

"Yes Aina, I will stay in the house always now and I will never go away again."

But after that, some guests came and Mahavir became busy again, leaving Aina feeling lonely again. It was a wonder that she was so lonely even in a crowd.

Chapter 3

That evening, Aina wore her best sari and went and stood near her favourite window where she could see the front courtyard and the steps leading to the old palace. Behind she could see the huge hall where the people would sit. People had started coming for the celebration. Suddenly there was a commotion and Aina saw that a palanquin had come, carried by two bearers. Out stepped a very pretty woman. Her lips were red with the betel leaf that she was still munching.

To the innocent Aina, this woman appeared to be a fairy. The woman was taken to a room on one side of the courtyard. Aina heard her father call out her name and Aina was delighted. She ran down the stairs hoping to be able to see the fairy, face to face. Seeing that her father was in a good mood, Aina took the opportunity to ask her father, "Can I see the fairy who has just come?"

Kalka nodded and took Aina to the dancing girl and said, "Bijli. She is Aina."

Bijli looked at Aina and said, "She is just as I thought she would be. She is very charming."

Aina said, "You are beautiful. May I touch you?"

Bijli caught her hand and pulled her close and said, "Ofcourse you can touch me, my lovely child."

Bijli embraced Aina who said, "You smell nice."

"I have put on some itra (perfume)," said she.

Kalka said, "Bijli, let her go now. Aina, go and get a drink and some snacks for this lady."

Aina went and said to her mother Gomti, "Ma. Papa has asked me to take some snacks and a drink for that Bijli who has just come in a palanquin."

Gomti's face became hard and unrelenting.

Gomti muttered, "Aina you let it be. I will go. Today I want to see what this great Bijli looks like."

Aina saw that no one was watching her, so she ran back to the room where the fairy was. Aina entered and stood staring at her as Bijli sat there alone.

The fairy looked up at her and smiled, saying, "Come here, child. You are a very lovely girl."

"But my mother says that I am dark and not fair like her, so I am not lovely," said Aina.

"Being fair is not necessary for being beautiful."

"So am I beautiful?" asked Aina.

"Ofcourse, my child, you are very beautiful," said the kind fairy as she embraced Aina.

"Nobody has told me that I am beautiful. Rather my mother says that I am bad and ugly," stated Aina.

"You cannot be bad and ugly. You look innocent, kind and good," answered the fairy.

"You are very nice and loving, more than my mother. I wish you were my mother," said Aina.

"Then think of me as your mother. But doesn't your mother love you?" asked the fairy.

"My mother doesn't love me. She loves Munna only. Are you my father's mistress?" asked Aina.

The question left Bijli dumbfounded. Bijli composed herself quickly and asked, "Who said this?"

"One of my aunts said this. I overheard her when she was telling another aunt. You know, I have lots and lots of aunts. There are so many people in our house. Are you Papa's mistress?" asked Aina.

Bijli asked, "Do you know the meaning of this word?"

Aina said, "No, but I think it means you are different. So can you cook food? Do you have children?"

"I have a daughter," said the fairy.

"Does she look like you?"

"Yes," said the fairy.

"Then she must be very beautiful."

"She is," said the fairy.

"But you never gave me an answer. Are you my father's mistress?" asked Aina.

Aina's mother Gomti had just entered, in time to hear the last sentence and she slapped Aina. But Aina was unfazed. Generally she was afraid of Gomti hitting her, but somehow she felt that, if her own mother hit her again, this fairy would save her. So Aina still stared at the woman in front of her, who was wearing wonderful clothes and a lot of jewellery. She was literally glowing.

Aina said, "You are pretty but my mother is more beautiful than you. Look at her. She has long hair and such big eyes. She looks like an angel when she smiles. You are not as fair as she is."

Gomti said, "I am sorry that Aina is being so rude. I will punish her for speaking like this to you."

The fairy said, "No please don't punish her. As it is she is a girl, and with the blessings of God, she will live to be a woman. In her life, being a woman, she will get enough punishment, tears and misery."

Gomti said, "But Bijli bai, it was unpardonable of her to speak such hurtful words to you."

Bijlee answered, "On the contrary, I feel that she is the first one who thought of me as an ordinary human being and as a mother. In our profession, we forget what we are and just remain an object for men's lust. I must say that it is also very nice that you are being so civil to me, otherwise we get disrespect from other women. I am obliged that you came personally to meet me. Thanks."

Aina said, "My mother is being polite because if she was rude to you, my father would beat her."

"Oh Lord! What do I do with this child?" said the exasperated Gomti.

"Does your husband beat you?" asked Bijli.

There was sympathy in her eyes for Gomti, and Gomti cringed. Gomti said, "He can do whatever he wants with me. He is my husband, married to me in the presence of society." Now Bijli seemed to wilt, as if an arrow had pierced her heart.

Aina felt that something was very wrong between her mother and the fairy. It made her feel uncomfortable and afraid. She tried to change the topic.

Aina asked, "Ma, give milk to me in this lovely glass that you have given this woman."

This time Gomti kept quiet and Bijli said bitterly, "You will not be allowed to use this glass, because no one in the house is supposed to drink from the glass that I have used. I am a dancing girl, so I am an outcaste. I actually belong to a very good family, but my fate is bad. Your name is Aina. Do you know what it means?"

"Yes. It means a mirror," said Aina.

In a brittle voice Bijli said, "So Aina, you must see that your mirror does not break like mine did. Mirrors are always fragile and when once there is a crack in the mirror, it is just thrown out as garbage. It has nothing but tears in its destiny, and tears hurt. Yes, they hurt a lot."

Aina's younger brother Munna, a twelve year old pampered, precocious but a fair and handsome boy, came running in just then and said in a rude manner, "Aaye Bijli. Come to sing in the hall."

Kalka walked in just as Munna spoke. Kalka looked very angry as he scolded his son, "Munna. Be polite. This is not how you should speak."

Aina said, "But Papa, this fairy is your mistress."

"How dare you, Aina!" said Kalka, advancing towards Aina with his hand raised.

"Let it be, please don't beat her," said Bijli, holding Aina tightly. Aina loved being protected and cuddled like that, but soon the fairy let her go.

Aina felt deprived as Bijli turned gracefully, her ankle bells jingling, and stepped out of the room.

Kalka muttered to his wife Gomti, "It is good that I have got a chance to talk to you. Both Aina and Munna have become very rude. Why don't you teach them good manners? What do you do the whole day? Take them in hand and see to it that they become well behaved."

"Why should I? Bijli is your passion. Ask her to mother your children," sneered Gomti bitterly.

Munna shouted, "She is not my mother. You are my mother. I don't want her to mother me."

"Ask your father about what he feels. He is not happy with one wife," said Gomti.

Kalka slapped Gomti hard, and said, "Shut up. You should not speak like this in front of our children.

Remain within your limits, you stupid woman. Get lost. Go to the women's quarters and don't come out."

Aina started crying and shouting, "Papa, why did you hit Ma? You do nothing but drink and now when you meet Ma, you just scold her and hit her."

But Kalka was no longer there to listen to the pain in his daughter Aina's voice as she sobbed. Aina heard him saying very gently to the fairy, "I am sorry they were rude. I hope you did not feel hurt."

Aina cried louder, "Ma, Papa has gone away."

But Gomti and Munna too had gone inside, and Aina was left alone. Aina sobbed, "Everyone leaves me. I am feeling scared. Oh! No one loves me."

Suddenly she was engulfed in a loving embrace and she realised that her fairy was holding her. The fairy said, "Stop crying Aina. Crying never helps. You have to help yourself. Be brave. You are strong inside in your heart. Aina, if you feel scared, other people will scare you more. Repeat this like a chant. 'I am brave. I depend on myself only. I will smile always.' When you tell your mind this, the mind will obey you and you will lose your fears and you will not be lonely. Be happy, my child. Promise me you will always smile, whatever happens."

Aina promised and the fairy said, "Good bye, my child. May God always look after you." And the fairy walked away towards the big hall where so many people were waiting for her. Just then her cousin Radha ran up and said, "Aina let us go and see the dance."

Aina ran after Radha to the outer hall, which was full of all their male relatives. Her cousins were serving snacks and drinks. They were also drinking. Then Bijli started singing and dancing gracefully.

Radha said, "Isn't she beautiful?"

Suddenly Aina screamed.

CHAPTER 4

Aina screamed because Prasad had caught her hand. He shouted, "Aina and Radha. What are you both doing here? This is no place for girls. Go and sleep."

Aina saw that Prasad Baba was also holding Radha's hand and Radha was looking terrified too. Prasad Baba was a terror for all the children.

Prasad Baba shouted at the women sitting behind a purdah, "You all are having fun. No one is bothered about these girls. Get these girls to bed. Everyone here just thinks of having fun."

An aunt got up and took Radha and Aina to the rooms behind, grumbling, "What pests you are! I have to miss out on such a beautiful song. Now go and sleep."

Aina and Radha did not feel bold enough to disobey Prasad Baba anymore. They quietly went to bed, whispering to each other, "Prasad Baba is so different from Mahavir Baba."

It was a fact. Mahavir was short and stout, while Prasad was tall and thin. Mahavir was a forgiving person who tolerated the inadequacies of others, quite opposite to Prasad who was a stern, unrelenting perfectionist and highly impatient with those who were weak. Mahavir just smiled away the quirks of those around him, while the angry Prasad gave them a piece of his austere mind. But though the two brothers were so different from each other, they shared a great rapport and understanding.

So Prasad went to his own room, leaving his elder brother Mahavir, sitting right in front of Bijli, with a glass of rum in his hand, listening to the beautiful lyrics being sung by her in her mellifluous voice. There was a reason for his presence there. Because alcohol was being served, he was afraid that the youngsters of the family might forget the line of decency. He knew that till he himself was present there, nobody could dare to misbehave with Bijli. And that is what happened.

Nearly the whole night, Bijli's dancing and singing continued, but as soon as Mahavir went to sleep, the youngsters started misbehaving. Under the influence of drinks, Raju caught Bijli's hand and Kalka became livid. He shouted, "Leave her alone. Get out." When he didn't, Kalka slapped Raju and sent him away.

Mahavir only came to know of this incident the next morning. It made him think and he saw to it that from that very day, life changed in the household. He called the culprits and scolded them severely. The boys were already going to school, now Mahavir ordered each of them to study at home too, for four hours daily. He told Prasad to monitor their studies and make them study hard. He curbed all the free fun times that the boys were used to. All the boys hated it, but they could not refuse.

The boys were not happy with Mahavir's dictat, but for Aina it was different. The presence of Mahavir was a god send for Aina. She felt comparatively secure now because her Mahavir Baba always protected her from everyone, even her mother, and now she felt happier as no one teased, scolded, bullied or hit her.

Only Munna troubled her, protected as he was by their mother Gomti. Aina could never understand why Gomti negated her presence and favoured Munna. It seemed that Gomti's world revolved only around him. There seemed to be no one else she cared for, not even her husband, for whom she had an obvious antipathy.

One day Munna started beating Aina when they accidentally tripped over each other. Aina started crying and calling for help, but Gomti did not respond. Then Aina slapped Munna who started yelling loudly. Gomti immediately came running to him. Gomti picked up Munna lovingly and said, "Why are you crying, my son?"

Munna said, "I did nothing but Aina slapped me."

Gomti slapped Aina at once, saying, "You are such a pest Aina. You always trouble Munna. Why didn't you die before you were born?"

This hurt Aina and she started crying. Gomti indifferently just walked away with Munna, leaving Aina alone. Tears slid helplessly down Aina's cheeks and she felt afraid and suddenly Aina's heart missed a beat. She started trembling as she heard a furtive sound behind her. As usual she felt as if someone was watching her, just waiting to pounce on her. She looked around but saw no one there. Then she thought of her grandfather.

CHAPTER 5

Aina ran towards the room of her grandfather, her only beacon of hope. He took her in his embrace and said, "Why have you been crying, Aina?"

Aina stated seriously, "Ma slapped me. She doesn't love me."

Mahavir said, "No Aina, your mother loves you. Aina you were born after a lot of prayers. For a long time Gomti had no children. Everyone taunted her that she was barren. You are her first child. Gomti was so happy, that she didn't leave you alone even for a second."

Aina said, "But now she doesn't care for me."

Mahavir said, "Aina, after your birth, people taunted Gomti that she had no son to carry on her family's name. So when Munna was born, Gomti was happy that she had given birth to a son and nobody could taunt her. So she gives all her time to Munna."

Aina said, "Doesn't she realize that I am left alone and neglected? It is always Munna this and Munna that. Yesterday she did not give me even one sweet while she gave them all to Munna. I felt so bad."

Coming into the room with a 'hookah' for her husband Mahavir, her grandmother Parwati said, "And, you stupid girl, you feel that the sweets should have been given equally to you and your brother Munna."

"Yes ofcourse, Daadi, everyone should be treated equally," said Aina to her grandmother Parwati.

She said, "No, Aina. Girls are supposed to give, and not take. In life you will need to adjust and therefore, from now you should have the habit of sacrifice."

"But that is not fair Daadi," replied Aina.

Her Baba said, "Fair or unfair. The boys are given the choicest things. Isn't that so, my dear wife?"

"Are you being sarcastic?" asked Parwati.

"Take it as you will, but the fact is that more importance is given to Munna, than to Aina. It is not right to make the girl suffer. She is extremely sensitive and vulnerable. She will soon start feeling deprived."

Daadi said, "Aina better become tough. Just now she is a real coward. Imagine, the other night she was crying and shrieking. How can she be so frightened?"

Mahavir looked a little annoyed with his wife. He said to her, "This is the first I am hearing about this. Aina, why didn't you tell me before?"

Aina said, "This is what I wanted to speak to you about Baba. I feel so scared. Many times it seems that someone is following me. Baba, I hear a heavy breathing and I feel that the person will hurt me."

"Oh! It is nothing but her mind making her dream of sordid things. She is a coward," said Daadi.

"No Daadi. Listen to me. A person does follow me actually and I hate it. I don't want to get hurt."

"Aina, it is just your overactive imagination. You better get your act together and become a flexible girl who can adjust anywhere. You will need to adjust in your in-law's place when you are married. Ask your Baba, how I lived my life. I was cloistered and inhibited with so many restrictions imposed by his mother," said Daadi.

Mahavir said, "That is all the more reason for you to show more concern towards the women of our family. Why are you making them suffer the same things that you had suffered? And you better let Aina alone."

Afraid that her grandparents may as usual start having an argument, Aina intervened, "Daadi, I feel afraid. Ma never stays near me. She doesn't care for me. I wish she loved me and I was special for her."

"Why do you think all these things? What has love got to do here? It is not important. You have been born in this family, everyone loves you anyway," said Daadi as she walked away to the inner courtyard.

"But Baba, I don't want to be loved anyway. I want to be special and important," said Aina tearfully.

"Then first love yourself Aina. Why do you cry so much? Child, stop crying or the world will make you cry more. Our country has become free but women are still shackled, specially in such a place as our Najapur. Here we still live in a conservative past while the world has moved to new things. I hope things improve for women. Tell me Aina. Who is stalking you?" asked her Baba.

"Baba, I can't make out who he is. I have often felt that someone is following me and is ready to hit me. I told Ma and Daadi about it, but they wouldn't believe me. No one believes me. Baba, do you believe me?"

Mahavir hugged Aina and said, "Ofcourse Aina. I believe you. Tell me what happens?"

"Since a long time I have heard the sound of footsteps and someone breathing behind me. After that many times someone actually grabbed at me, but I was always able to run away," explained Aina.

Mahavir was really perturbed. He said, "All right, to take precautions, from today you sleep in our room."

"Thank you Baba. I would love that," said Aina relieved that at last someone had been kind to her.

"Aina, listen carefully. From now on don't go near men, even if they are from the family," said Baba.

"But Baba, you are also a man and you are also family!"

Mahavir burst out laughing saying, "That is why your Daadi says that you are incorrigible."

That night Aina slept in the room of her Baba and Daadi. She was happy, but suddenly she heard someone outside. Her heart started pounding when she heard the footsteps coming closer. She screamed as all of a sudden she started feeling that someone was throttling her. She felt as if she could not breathe.

"Aina. Get up. Wake up child. You are seeing a nightmare. There is no one here except me. You are safe. Tell me what happened," said Baba.

Aina looked around and saw that only her Baba was there. She said in a relieved tone, "Baba. Thank God it was not happening. Tonight it may have been a nightmare, but it happens often."

"Aina, you are getting nightmares because of your fears. Who can want to hurt you? No outsider stays in the house. All these are our relatives. How can they hurt you? The servants also sleep outside the house. Then why is this happening to you only? No other girl has complained of being followed. But I still believe you. If you remember anything you must tell me."

"Thank God, Baba that you believe me. I love you Baba," said Aina.

Mahavir's voice broke as he hugged her and said, "I believe you and I understand your fear. If anything happens ever again, you must tell me. If I find that horrible man, I will thrash him. Now no one can trouble you, Aina. I want you to be very brave. You have to fight this out. Give it back to the scoundrel. If you don't like him, chuck him away. Make him cry. You don't cry."

"I know I should not cry, but I feel like crying."

Mahavir explained, "That is normal but just take a deep breath and visualize something beautiful, then you will not cry. Promise me that you will always show a strong will power. A woman has the potential to become anything. Treat her well and she will shower devotion. Hurt her, and in case she feels the injustice, and is bold and brave, she will be the greatest enemy ever."

Aina said, "Baba. I will remember this and try to be such a fearless woman. When you are there with me, I feel brave and feel that I can do anything. Please Baba, you won't leave me alone ever, will you?"

Mahavir caught the poor child in his embrace and soothed her fears. She clung to him with all the might possible in her slim frame, mortally afraid that this security could be snatched away from her. Even in such a short life, she had come to expect the worst to happen to her always. Would she ever be able to shed this corroding knot of fear from her heart?

CHAPTER 6

Aina was now happy as her Baba was with her. The more her parents negated her existence, the more Aina's world centred around her Baba. He was thus the only person closest to Aina. She loved her Baba more now, because he was the only one to give her the special attention that her heart craved. And Mahavir was full of life. He changed the whole world of Aina. There were many restrictions on the girls, but Aina was lucky that she was exempted from many of them because of Mahavir. Except Prasad no one dared to say anything to Aina because she had Mahavir's support.

One morning Aina was sent by her mother to give the betel box to Kalka. Aina walked out to the male quarters, and then she again felt as if someone was coming after her. She felt paralysed with fear as she heard footsteps behind her. The footsteps came closer and closer. She wanted to run but she could not. The footsteps came right behind her and she felt two strong hands catch her from behind and a funny voice said, "Grrrrr. You stupid girl, I will teach you a lesson."

Two hands tried to pick her up from behind. That made her flail her arms and kick her legs which hit the person's stomach hard. His hold on her slackened. She took the chance to get out of his hold. Not daring to stay even a minute more, she ran from there to Mahavir and clung to him screaming, "Save me Baba. That man is after me again. He wanted to teach me a lesson."

Mahavir asked her the details. She could not tell him who the man was. Mahavir held and comforted her and told her that he would look after her. He tried to analyse who it could have been. He thought of the many young men in their joint family who could have been the culprit. He tried to understand what could be the cause.

He started thinking that someone could have a grudge against Aina. But she was just a child. Then he felt it possible that Aina was being used to take revenge from him because Aina was his favourite. He recollected past instances. He remembered scolding all the young men for misbehaving with Bijli. It could be any of them.

Mahavir also thought of why this was happening to Aina only when there were so many girls in the family. Was it because she was less protected by her own parents? Whatever, he decided to keep alert and watchful, so that he could catch the culprit.

He took care of Aina, but one day she was sent up to the terrace for an errand by Gomti and Raju was there. This time Sabal was not there to save her.

Raju shouted, "You stupid girl, I will throw you down. Your father slapped me. Your grandfather favours you all the time. I cannot bear it any more. I hate you."

Aina saw Girish standing on the terrace, alone, away from the others, deep in thought. She thought that he would scold Raju, but Girish just looked away. Raju was coming towards her angrily and Aina got scared and ran off. She ran straight to her Baba and said, "Baba, Raju just got angry at me and said that you favour me. I ran away because he said he would throw me down from the terrace. And Baba, Girish Chacha said nothing. He is the son of Prasad Baba, isn't it? Why does Girish Chacha remain so angry, lonely and sad all the time?"

"Girish loved a girl but we refused to let him marry that girl because she was of a caste lower than ours. So he is angry with us," said Baba.

Aina said, "Baba. Let him marry that girl."

"It is not possible now as that particular girl has been married already to someone else," said Mahavir.

"Oh Baba! You should have let him marry that girl, then he would have been happy. Raju's brother Hari also married out of our caste and you let him," said Aina.

"Girish wanted to marry that girl a long time back when everyone was very strict about these things. By the time Hari married, things had changed. Still we had refused to accept Hari too, but we were forced to agree."

Mahavir still felt that he had done the right thing in not permitting Girish to marry into a lower caste. How could he explain to Aina that he was the head of the joint family, who had a duty to uphold the traditions of his forefathers. He felt bad that after denying Girish, he could not stop Hari from marrying Bela. Mahavir knew that this must have irked Girish more, and that is why hurt and anger were still smouldering within Girish.

CHAPTER 7

Some nights later, Aina could hear someone outside. She was still sleeping in the room of Mahavir and Parwati. Suddenly she heard someone breathing deeply again. She checked if that uneven breathing was her Baba's or Daadi's. But no, she could make out a third breathing and she felt paralysed with fear. Who was outside? Then she heard footsteps coming towards her, closer and closer and she screamed. Mahavir and Parwati ran to her. Aina seemed very upset and scared.

Mahavir checked outside, but found no one there. He then saw that Aina couldn't sleep. Parwati went to sleep, but Mahavir bolted the door from inside and started telling Aina stories about their ancestors.

Baba said, "There was one ancestor whose sycophants made him believe that he was invincible and that nothing and nobody could kill him. So when guns came into the market, he ordered for one. He could not believe that such a small bullet could kill a giant of a man like him. One day he asked his servant to fire point blank at him with the gun, because he was so sure that he would not die. The trembling servant would himself have been killed if he had not obeyed. So the poor servant fired the gun and the great hero gladly faced the bullet, but unfortunately he died. This is a true story."

Tears welled up in her eyes as she said, "Why do people die?"

"That is the way of this world. There has to be a balance of life and death in all living beings. When old people go, then only new people come. So no tears, Aina. They lived and died. Death is inevitable. If people had not died before us, maybe we would not have been born. That is life. Accept it and don't cry."

"But Baba. How will I manage if you die?" said Aina, and she cried uncontrollably.

Baba hugged her and assured her, "You will manage. God will give you the will power. When God gives pain, he also gives the strength to face that pain."

Aina suddenly caught his hand feverishly and whispered furiously, "Baba listen. I can hear that heavy breathing again. It is not Daadi's breathing. That man will take me away from you. Oh Baba! Save me from him."

Mahavir was shocked at Aina's pallor. He quickly went out to check the corridor outside his room. He could not see anyone in the dark. Yet he was serious when he came back, because he had heard a heavy breathing too, but he had not been able to see anyone around. He shut the door and bolted it. Mahavir showed Aina as if nothing had happened but he started recalling who amongst the youngsters breathed heavily.

Then he realized that it would be hard to say because many old and young members of the family suffered from asthma which he believed was a genetic family malady, which was aggravated because of the smoke pollution from the nearby factory.

He started talking again to Aina, "We had a very intelligent horse. He would cross the road himself to drink water from the trough. We just had to say, "Go to the station" and he would take us to the railway station.

And once he saved my life. We were driving out of the city, when the horse stopped. We found out that the bridge in front had been swept away by a sudden flood. If the horse had not stopped, I might have been killed."

"Baba? Someone is outside again. Didn't you hear anything? Maybe he is looking for me," said Aina.

With alacrity belying his age, Mahavir rushed to the door, opened it and looked out. He did not see anyone but he started shouting, "Hari, Kalka, Prasad, help. There is a thief here." He ran down the corridor.

The dawn was just showing its blushing face, so there was some light now. He saw a sleeve behind a pillar. He rushed as fast as he could towards it, but the sleeve moved. He then saw someone dash away and go around the corner. He ran, but by the time he reached the corner, there was no one there.

He went to check if the outer doors had been closed. They were still locked from inside. There had been some man there. He was sure of it, because he had seen the back of the person with his own eyes. Aina had been right. Someone was stalking her. Aina had not imagined it. The man must have been looking for Aina in the room where she used to sleep with the other girls of the family. Maybe he did not know that Aina was now sleeping in their room, so he was prowling around.

All the men came running at his call, but they saw no intruder. "That means it was someone within the house," thought Mahavir and he became very worried about Aina, but he never said anything to her. He checked the young men who had come. All of them were present. But then the young man who was the culprit, could have got the time to run back and join the other male members of the family in the corridor.

He told everyone to go to sleep and then he came to his room. Daadi was holding Aina who was crying and then Aina said, "Who do you think wants to hurt me? Whom did you see outside?"

Mahavir caressed her hair and replied, "A ghost. And the ghost said that Aina is beautiful, so it comes to look at Aina. And do you know, the ghost is very fat."

Daadi said to her husband, "You must have seen a mirror."

Aina burst out laughing and both of them tried to put her to sleep. Aina was restless and she suddenly said, "What if that man kills me? Everything will end. Where do we go after death?"

"I don't know, Lady. I have never died before," said Baba laughingly. They kept her distracted by telling her funny stories and finally Aina slept. Then Mahavir and Parwati discussed who the person could be.

"Why would anybody be after Aina?"

Mahavir said thoughtfully, "It could be that someone is taking revenge from me. They might be targetting Aina as they know that Aina is my favourite." Daadi said, "Why would he prowl for so long?"

Mahavir said, "He is probably being so obvious on purpose to make me aware that he is after Aina. Who could it be? The figure I saw was of a young man, so all the young men are suspects. The problem is that most of them have reasons to carry a grudge against me. But who ever he is, I won't let him frighten Aina any more. I will confront all these boys first thing in the morning."

Parwati replied quickly, "No. Don't do that. If it is proved to be true, then life will become uncomfortable for all of us. Moreover our relations with that boy's family may get strained. You must not talk about this at all."

CHAPTER 8

The next morning Mahavir took a decision after deep thought. Mahavir called Prasad and said, "I think our boys should study in Lucknow if they want to do well in future, because there are better schools and colleges there. You can send even Sabal to start his law practice in that city. Tell Girish to take a job in the city and take a house there. Then all the boys can live with him."

Prasad obeyed. He and his family didn't even think of questioning his brother's decision, though Girish did not want to shift to Lucknow. But ultimately Girish was as obedient as usual, and he started applying for a job in Lucknow. Prasad sent a man to arrange for a comfortable accommodation in Lucknow for the boys.

Finally Prasad told Mahavir, "Girish has got a good job in Lucknow but the parents of many boys and young men don't want to send their boys to Lucknow."

"Don't force them," remarked Mahavir.

Within a month, Om, Som, Girish, Gittoo, Raju, Sabal and Prabal had been sent to Lucknow. Soon, the young gentlemen had been made comfortable in a house in Lucknow, with a servant, financed by Mahavir and managed by Girish. Mahavir then heaved a sigh of relief. Now the boys would be well educated from good schools and colleges and with that, there would be no reason for Aina to be scared as no one would bully her.

Now he waited to see if Aina complained again. When Aina did not complain for quite some time, it was confirmed that the 'breathing' terror of Aina had actually stopped. This made Mahavir sad, because it meant that one of these boys was the culprit, who had been stalking Aina. He actually suspected one of them, but he kept quiet as he had no proof. He decided to keep an eye on that particular boy whenever he came back home.

Now Aina was better, but she still continued to have nightmares in which she would wake up drenched in sweat, trembling like a leaf. Mahavir tried to be there for her whenever she needed him, as he saw that the nightmares were so real, that Aina would wake up believing that she was being chased and beaten.

Aina said one day, "I miss Sabal chacha."

"But it is important for him to finish his law course," answered Mahavir.

"Baba, then why don't you send me to school?"

"Aina. You are a girl. How will studies help you? Girls have to get married, so you have to marry and go to your in-law's house. You don't need studies for that."

"But I want to study like Munna," said Aina.

"You will do nothing of the sort, Aina. Learn how to manage the house. That will help you more."

"But that will not let me earn money," said Aina.

Mahavir was shocked. He exclaimed, "Are you off your head, young lady? Are all the male members dead that you are thinking of earning money? We will get you married as soon as we find a good boy for you. Till then I am there to provide for you."

Prasad was sitting there. He said, "I think you should send her to school. When she gets distracted, then she will not get nightmares."

Mahavir said, "No, I don't think that is the right thing to do. If she has a bad experience outside with no one to protect her, then she might suffer more."

Aina started pestering Mahavir to send her to school, but in this her Baba would just not listen to her. So one day when the postman brought a letter, Aina couldn't read it. Most of the male members were not in the house. Aina took the postcard letter inside to the woman's quarters. The women were not educated.

They saw that one corner of the postcard was torn. They started crying. Just then Mahavir came back with Kalka. They got worried on hearing the women crying because a letter with one torn corner had come.

Mahavir said, "Oh! That means it is a letter informing about someone's death. Kalka, read it quickly."

Kalka read the letter and said, "Pitaji. This is really sad. My sister Radhapyari's youngest son Umesh, is no more. He was only fifteen years old."

Stronger wails of sorrow filled the palace again for well nigh three hours. It was decided that Kalka and Mahavir would go to the funeral, and they started their preparations to go. Just as they were about to leave, there was a commotion outside and someone shouted, "Ghost, ghost. Run away. Help! Help!"

Then Umesh, the supposedly dead boy, walked in.

Mahavir said, "Umesh, you are alive! We received a letter that you had died."

Umesh replied, "The letter was sent because a crow sat on me. My grandmother strongly believed in the superstition that I could die because of it, as crows sit on dead bodies. So to remove this ill omen, she forced my father to write to you that I had died.

Because postcards with the news of a death have one corner torn, so my grandmother tore one corner of it. My mother sent me here, because she knew that you all would be worried."

"Thank God," said Mahavir and life in the palace slipped back to its normal routine, except for Aina who saw a nightmare of ghosts. She said to her Baba, "I am afraid of even one ghost. If I die then how will I manage alone up in the sky where there will be so many ghosts?"

Mahavir replied seriously, "I will be there to receive you. I will tell God that I cannot leave my Aina alone and He will send me to you. In this way you will have me near you always to protect you."

CHAPTER 9

Life went on, with some changes. The women were kept busy in their everyday chores and fasts, but there were frequent celebrations now, as everyday seemed to be a festival in the house, because of the sanguine temperament of Mahavir. Yet Aina noticed that the men and the boys mainly enjoyed life, because the women and the girls had to do all the cooking and housework. She felt bad that the girls were not allowed to study at home or go to school. Girls had to lead a very cloistered life. It seemed that there was a desperation in the elders to get the girls married as early as possible.

Aina had now started looking charming and attractive, despite her dusky complexion, and soon her grandmother often talked about her marriage.

She said to her grandmother one day, "Why get me married so soon? When were you married Daadi?"

Daadi said, "I was married when I was nine years old."

Baba started laughing, "Do you know Aina, on the day of the wedding, your Daadi had gone to sleep and someone had to pick her up and take her around the sacred fire behind me. The next day, she fought with me for sweets. She also wanted to fly kites with us."

"But why was she married so early Baba?"

Daadi explained, "These early marriages are done because a girl is a liability and a burden."

"Daadi girls are not liabilities," said Aina.

"Watch this Granny giving me a lecture," said Daadi which meant that the subject was closed.

As time passed, Aina became taller. Her mother and grandmother sent her proposal to different boys, but no proposal was accepted. Aina was not bothered about this, though she was fast slipping through the blush of adolescence, yet protected by her Baba as she was, she was oblivious to the vagaries of life outside her own inhibited world of innocence, where the external world did not intrude. She was slowly fighting with her fears.

Still she was not aware that she had got shapely curves. She would have been surprised if anyone had told her that she looked extremely attractive with her smooth dusky complexion moulded into sharp features, illumined by her sparkling expressive brown eyes and long hair. All Aina could think of was, that she was not fair and lovely like her mother, so she was not beautiful.

Then one day an astrologer Swami Ram came. He was reading the palms of the men.

Gomti said, "Aina. Go and tell your Baba to have Munna's palm read by Swami Ram."

Aina went and relayed the message to her Baba. As she was turning to go back inside, Swami Ram shouted, "Wait here girl. Show me your hand."

Aina obediently spread out her hands. Swami Ram said in his loud voice, "Oh my poor girl! What a painful destiny awaits you! There will be such great catastrophes in your life! You can never get happiness, because you are totally in the hands of Fate. You will be rich, but you will suffer terribly. You will suffer pain."

"Hey! Swami. Just stop it, you hypocrite," came the voice of Prasad, "Swami, just get out of here. How dare you make such predictions and scare her? Get up Swami. No one will show their palms to you."

Before anyone could say anything, Prasad had driven the raging astrologer out of the palace. Aina felt afraid at what the swami had said. Mahavir saw Aina looking worried. He took her outside and said, "Aina let us walk outside in our front courtyard for some time."

Mahavir asked Aina, "Why are you so worried about what the swami said? He could be wrong."

"Baba, the Swami said that I will suffer, but how will I face the sufferings?" asked Aina.

Mahavir told her, "I wish you never suffer in life but even if you do, it depends on you whether you suffer or not. The action may be in the hands of fate or other people, but your reaction is in your hands. Just have a positive reaction and there will be no suffering. For that, just believe in yourself and celebrate life regardless. No one can help you till the intention and motivation comes from within you. You can do it Aina. I trust you."

But for the first time Aina was not consoled by her Baba's words. She remembered the Swami's words and there was an ominous foreboding whenever she even thought of her future. What would the future hold for her? What were the calamities that she would have to face? She shivered with fright and nervousness.

CHAPTER 10

A<small>S</small> time passed, her essential temperament did not change, but as she was more grown up now, she started understanding the disturbing nuances of life and relationships. Aina tried to please and appease all the relatives of the family also, because she hated conflict, but her immediate family had always been Aina's world and now she understood them better. She knew now that her Mahavir Baba too was not infallible as she had believed. He could be stubborn and conventional though he often talked about freedom being given to women.

Aina had been more afraid of Parwati, her Daadi (grandmother) always, because Daadi was very strong in mind. Daadi was quite a volatile character. Her long nose was denotive of her strong emotions. The tip of her nose would wobble when she was near to tears. Often when her nose grew fiery red, the children around her charged away to safety, afraid of a sharp whack from her, because she had a terrible temper. Rukmini once told Aina an incident that had happened with Parwati.

One night, before sleeping, Parwati had told her son Kalka to bolt all the doors, otherwise the daughters-in-law of the house would disturb her in the morning (as it was a custom that all the daughters-in-law touched the elder women's feet every morning). The next morning, Parwati woke up and saw three women with their heads covered. She felt so furious, that she stuck out her feet and said angrily, "Come touch my feet and go away at once." The three touched her feet and went away.

Then Parwati shouted for her son Kalka. When he came running, she said, "Why did you disobey me? I am angry with you. I had told you to bolt all the doors as I did not want to be disturbed in the morning."

Kalka checked and said, "All the bolts are still closed. No one could have come inside."

Parwati then nonchalantly said, "Call the priest to find out if there are spirits in the house."

The priest was called and he told them that there were three spirits in the box room.

Rukmini had ended the story by saying, "That is why we never go into the boxroom alone."

Aina laughed, "Daadi's temper had probably scared the spirits enough to make them touch her feet."

But now Aina realized that Daadi had a soft side to her nature also, which she hid behind her usual brusque demeanour. Baba, was not the cranky despot in their house, because this role was played by Daadi, who was the home commander who ruled strictly, her hawk eyes registering each and every movement of the family members. Aina was often perplexed that in every way the women of the family had to obey the men, but Daadi was above that law. She managed the finances of the family and everyone had to bend to her will, but to her credit, she was fair and impartial in her dealings.

Aina now knew that her Daadi and Baba were consistently at loggerheads but there was an underlying concern for each other. They had arguments, with Daadi going on a silent strike for some days, till her husband apologized, yet they could not do without each other.

As time passed, the orders of Mahavir and Parwati were still obeyed by everyone, but money had started to matter because there was a dearth of it, as the income was becoming less, but the expenses were more. Many family members stopped giving their earnings to Parwati, though they enjoyed all the benefits.

Aina saw her Baba helping people, but in return getting only ingratitude. And slowly the grandeur of their lives was dying out because it was getting harder to manage financially. Aina was worried that Baba often looked tense. As a result he started becoming more preoccupied and had less time for Aina. Moreover circumstances had given a lot of wear and tear to the tapestry of their daily life. Relationships were the first casualty. Aina realized that there were chinks of underlying misunderstandings and conflicts which were slowly causing irreparable animosity in the family.

Aina seethed at the change in her joint family but still her world was the immediate family of Mahavir and Prasad. She was still afraid of Prasad, but his young wife, whom Aina called Rukmini Amma, had become like a friend to her. Aina now had come to know that Rukmini was actually the second wife of Prasad. The first wife had died while giving birth to the eldest son Girish.

Prasad had been forced to marry again. Rukmini had been quite young when she came into this family. She got along famously with everybody and she was a breath of fresh air in the stuffy, overcrowded palace. But at times Aina caught Rukmini Amma crying, though she would never tell her why she was crying.

Aina still heard taunts from her mother, because, all of a sudden, Gomti became obsessed with getting Aina married off. She would scream at Aina, "You are growing up like a tree but no one is ready to marry you. The family says I don't care about getting you married. What can I do if you are dark and ugly?"

This repeated tirade snubbed whatever spirit and confidence Aina had. She was also disturbed about her father's excessive drinking. His nocturnal visits to Bijli's house were still a regular feature and there was a coldness still in his association with his wife Gomti! Aina's younger brother Munna was growing up to be quite a bully, so Aina did not get on well with him. With the lessening of her Baba's attention towards her, Aina felt a vacuum inside her. She felt a yearning for love.

CHAPTER 11

One day Mahavir was reclining in his huge wooden armchair. Just then Rukmini Amma came with a veil on her head and signalled to Aina to give the glass of tea to him. Aina had noticed that Rukmini Amma had started coming towards the men's area, but she still never spoke directly to Baba.

"Why do women cover their heads?" said Aina, falling into her routine of asking questions.

Baba said, "Aina this is because of the 'purdah' system (cloister). It is a custom from our past. Women went out, in veils in covered palanquins only so that no one could see them. This purdah was to protect them from males, specially the people who had invaded India. Even inside the house there was purdah."

"Was grandmother beautiful before marriage?"

"I don't know. I first saw her face when she was the mother of two of my children, then she was pretty."

"Why Baba? Why didn't you see her before?"

"I didn't have a separate room then, and your Daadi did not stay in my room. We were not supposed to see our wives in front of others, neither talk to them in public. They always covered their faces like now."

"Then how were children produced?" asked Aina, who retained her artlessness.

Baba replied, "Hush child. If anyone heard you speaking so openly, you will be punished. But to answer your question, there used to be a room where couples used to meet, like the mating room we have here."

"But what if the wrong lady came in?"

"It happened once with me. I had taken sweets for your grandmother. In the dark I saw her sitting there. She ate the sweets and I asked her, "Did you like them?" When she recognized my voice she screamed and ran away from the room. She was my younger brother Prasad's first wife. Thank God I spoke when I did."

Aina burst out laughing. She said, "Baba. You mean to say that you never saw your wife's face."

Baba smiled and said, "Yes, and I did not recognize her for quite some time. Once we went to the 'Kumbh Mela' (Fair) in Allahabad. In the middle of the crowd one day, my mother said, "Mahavir. Where is your wife?" We looked around but she was nowhere there. I hadn't seen her face till then. I just remembered that she had been wearing a green sari. So I went to a woman in green and picked her up. I brought her to my mother and asked, "Is she my wife?" But she wasn't. Like that I brought five more women dressed in green. Thankfully the fifth one was your grandmother. But by then the families of the other women were after my blood."

"What did you do to save yourself, Baba?"

"I was a very fast runner. I ran and stopped only when I reached where we were staying," said he.

Aina laughed, imagining her stoutly built grandfather running away with four families after him.

The story Mahavir was telling Aina had to be stopped, as just then the family barber came and Mahavir had a long chat with him. Mahavir then told Aina, "Munna will soon be married. There is a proposal.

A barber from that family will come to see Munna and then his marriage will be fixed."

Aina went and asked her mother, "Why is Munna being married when I am not married?"

"You are shameless!" said her mother.

"Munna is younger than me and still in school."

"He has got a very good proposal from a very good family. We can't say no. The girl's family is very wealthy," said her Ma.

"But I am elder and a girl. I should be married first," said Aina.

"This is being done for you only, you stupid girl. The dowry that Munna will get, will be given to you. We are no longer rich. We are having a problem fixing your marriage because we don't have money to give as a dowry. I will be glad when you get married," said Ma.

"Do you hate me so much? Am I a burden on you?" asked Aina tearfully.

"All girls have to be married. That is the ultimate for any girl. But I don't know what is written in your destiny. Why did you have to be born with such a dark skin?" said her Ma.

Aina said, "Papa is dark, so what can I do?"

Just then her father came saying, "I am acting in a play. All of you can come to see the play today."

"You know that we are not allowed to go outside," said Gomti sullenly.

Kalka said, "I have asked both Mother and Father. They have allowed you all. Mother is coming with us and we will all go in carriages and Father says that there is no need to cover the carriages."

Aina cheered. Everyone dressed up and Daadi was the most eager to see her son perform on stage. They went to the theatre and Aina looked around the big hall with the high stage, with a curtain in front. Before the stage, sat the musicians who would play the background music and who would accompany the actors with the orchestra when they sang. And then the play began.

Aina realized that not a single woman was acting on the stage and that young boys were playing the roles of women. Suddenly the villain Bagla Bhagat came onto the stage. Aina was surprised that the villain Bagla Bhagat's role was being acted out by her own father. As per his role, he started teasing the women on the stage. He did it so well that even Aina started feeling angry with her father. All the women in the hall began saying nasty things about Bagla Bhagat.

Suddenly Daadi's long nose began wobbling.

Aina stiffened as she saw the nose becoming red. What would Daadi do now? Daadi had become very angry that all the women were cursing her son.

Daadi turned around and started shouting, "Shut up all of you. Don't you dare say a word about my son."

She even slapped a woman who was saying, "May Bagla Bhagat rot in hell."

After the play, Kalka came to meet them and Daadi shouted at him, "Why do you do such roles? Everyone was cursing you."

He said, "If they were cursing me, it means that I am a good actor."

Daadi said, "I will never come to see you acting. I can't bear to see people cursing you."

After that Daadi never went to see a play in which her son Kalka acted.

CHAPTER 12

Though Daadi was the most respected of all the family members, but many were ready to rebel because of her autocratic arrogance. Even Mahavir himself rebelled sometimes. He was not supposed to have sweets, but he would eat sweets on the sly. And Aina had heard people whispering that Mahavir Baba also had a prostitute as a keep. Aina couldn't believe it.

Since her Baba had come to stay in the palace, Aina knew that her grandfather used to go out on many nights. Maybe he used to visit a prostitute. Aina never had the guts to ask her grandfather about it to verify the rumours, but one day she asked her grandmother, "Daadi where does Grandpa often go in the night?"

"What has that got to do with you?" said Daadi sharply.

"It does. I do not like our neighbours talking that he goes to a prostitute," said Aina.

"So what is wrong with that?" Aina really wondered if Daadi was not at all affected. Her tone showed no emotion, but her long nose wobbled.

Aina said, "I would never let my husband go to another woman."

"How dare you talk about your marriage!"

Aina said boldly, "Daadi, you don't speak about it, but I am sure you feel bad that grandfather goes to another woman." Daadi was quiet, though her nose became absolutely red, and when Aina thought that she would not talk any more, Daadi said in a choked serious voice, "We are women, Aina. We are not supposed to have a heart or a soul. We are not supposed to think or feel. We are just supposed to be silly automatons who accept what our lord and master makes us do. These men! They are the cause of so much heartburn, yet we have to serve them like bonded slaves."

"Why do you accept it?" questioned Aina.

"What can we do? If they turned us out, where would we go?" asked Daadi.

"Go to your brother's house, Daadi," said Aina.

"My brother's wife would not like my living there for more than a few days, Aina," said Daadi.

"You could marry again," said Aina.

"Girl! Are you mad? What has got into you to talk like this? We marry for keeps. You stop yourself, lady. This is not how girls should think even, let alone talk."

Then Daadi fell quiet. After a few moments she said, as if speaking aloud, "We women cannot remarry. We cannot run away. We just have to bear whatever comes in our lives. It is all destiny. And we have to accept it without a word. So Aina, stop thinking and speaking all this. It will hurt you less, if you just tow the line these men make for you."

"But women suffer so much, Daadi."

"Yes. They suffer trauma and agony and there is no reprieve. We women are puppets in the hands of these men, though they don't deserve it. Yes, it hurts that your grandfather goes out. But what can I do? Men can do anything they want, but a woman has to be pure. Men can look at any woman and get away with it, but a woman would be flogged publicly or ostracized, if she dared even look at someone. We women are like dainty mirrors. We have to keep our virtuous reputation in tact, otherwise the slightest crack on it would rupture its purity and we would be faced with humiliation and shame."

"But Daadi, why should we bear all this? I don't like being a girl. I can't accept or tolerate like you all do. I feel so trapped." Aina burst out crying.

"Stop crying, Aina. Stock the tears in your eyes because you have a lifetime to spend them," said Daadi gruffly, patting her clumsily because she was already regretting talking to Aina in this manner. What if Aina became a rebel? She would then have to suffer a fate worse than hell in her in-law's house.

She said, "Aina, just forget what I have said. Remember that your Baba lets me do what I want in the house. May you get a husband who respects you, but remember Aina, you have to obey whatever the elders decide. You have to obey your in-laws and husband."

Aina retorted, "But Daadi, why can't women be free to do what they want to do? Why should men have all the privileges and women have just sufferings?"

Daadi answered, "It is just our kismet, our fate!"

CHAPTER 13

The next day changed Aina's mood as it proved to be very exciting. Her father was doing another play. He took them to the theatre again. But it was a very sad play because it was about lovers who met with a tragedy in the end. Aina felt glad that Daadi had refused to come to see the play, because this time her father was playing the villainous role of the father, who would not let his son marry his beloved. The last scene was the most tragic as the lovers decided to end their lives because they couldn't marry. They shouted 'Farewell' to each other and started falling down. And the audience cried.

But soon the tragedy turned to comedy. Probably they had to fall down as the music ended, but the music did not end, so the two lovers straightened up again. Strangely, this happened many times. The two would say 'Farewell' and start falling down, then bob up again, while the music continued to play with gusto, the same notes again and again. Soon it became quite funny. The two beloveds saying 'Farewell' repeatedly, and as soon as they prepared to slip down dead, the two would spring up again. And the music went on playing the same boisterous notes. It was so amusing that the audience forgot the tears and ended up in splits.

Then the theatre people decided to find out the reason for this. The theatre director looked at the band of musicians sitting between the audience and the stage, and he saw that the musicians were sitting in a state of terror, because in front of the harmonica, a cobra snake was sitting with its hood open, ready to strike.

So in his fright of the snake, the man playing the harmonica was not stopping the music. He played on and on, to keep the snake moving to the rhythm of the music, so that it would not bite him.

Everyone started shouting 'Snake. Snake.' The audience in the front row started running away, but the musicians went on playing the same tune and the two lovers kept on saying 'Farewell' and bobbing up again and again. Finally a man went and caught the snake and took it away. What probably had attracted the snake to crawl inside the hall from the garden outside was, that the harmonica was playing the tune like a 'Been' which was an instrument used to mesmerize snakes.

The reason for the bobbing figures was that a stage hand had been sitting backstage to lower the platform which would take the lovers down into the pit. He could not see the stage but he had to lower the ropes in his hand when the music stopped. As the music did not stop, he did not lower the platform, and so the hero and heroine would bob up again. Now when the music finally stopped, the backstage man lowered the ropes and the platform went down. Finally the lovers on the stage said 'Farewell' and fell down with the music dying slowly, with a last crescendo as the lovers fell.

Aina loved the laughter all around her, for she hated tragedies and this snake interlude had made the stark tragedy into a sheer comedy.

They returned home and Aina related the comic incident to her Daadi and they all laughed heartily. That night when everyone was asleep, a postman brought a telegram. The men were sleeping and so the telegram was received by a servant. He called out, "Open the door. A telegram has come." Aina was awake as she always had a problem sleeping in the night. She heard the servant. She recognized the voice of the servant saying, "There is a telegram for your Baba."

Aina took the telegram and went to Baba's room, but he was not there. Just then her 'bua' (aunt) Radhapyaari, who had come to spend some time with them, got up for a glass of water.

Aina went to her and said, "Bua, a telegram has come."

Radhapyaari said, "What! A telegram? Oh my Lord!" and she wailed very loudly leaving Aina quite shaken and she started crying. All the women who heard her, came running down to see what had happened and hearing about the telegram, all the ladies started crying.

Prasad came and said, "What is the commotion about?"

"A telegram has come," said Rukmini, because the other ladies would not speak in front of him.

"So why are they crying?" asked Prasad.

His wife Rukmini said, "Because a telegram must mean that someone has died."

Prasad said, "Did someone read it?"

"We all can't read," replied Rukmini.

Prasad then read the telegram and said, "Stop crying. Radhapyaari. Let us have some sweets. Your son Umesh has come first in Middle school."

All the tears dried up within seconds as everyone rejoiced and Gomti and Rukmini distributed sweets to all the members of the family.

Aina said, "All this crying happened because no one could read. I wish we were allowed to study."

Prasad said, "You are right Aina, but the elders will not permit that and we have to obey them."

The next day the barber came. Then the barber gave a marriage proposal for Munna and Mahavir replied, "We heartily agree to this proposal."

There were happy congratulations all around.

The dates for Munna's engagement also were finalised. The initial festivities of the engagement filled up the next month. A feast was given and there was a lot of merriment, till everything got forgotten as a veritable storm overcame the family, shaking the very roots.

CHAPTER 14

Aina would never forget that night. Her father Kalka and grandfather had dressed up with a lot of care. Daadi told Aina that they had been invited by Nawab Hajmat Miya of Anosi, who had come to Najapur to stay. He had arranged a feast to meet all the elite people.

It was a great honour to be invited to his palace. So her Baba and Papa were going to the house of the Nawab for a party where a beautiful dancing girl was to sing and dance. She was the greatly acclaimed Munni Bai whom they had never seen before, who was said to be the mistress of the Nawab.

Prasad told Kalka, "Don't go to the Nawab's palace because my organisation is taking out a protest march against the dancing by a nautch girl."

Kalka went and told Mahavir about it, who thought over it and then called Prasad.

Mahavir said, "Prasad, we have to go because, if we don't, the Nawab will feel bad."

"But I will be taking out a procession with black flags," said Prasad.

Mahavir said, "It will be a peaceful procession, won't it? Then you do your job and let Kalka and I honour our commitment to the Nawab."

It was later that same night that Aina was sleeping in her room when she heard many people crying loudly. In a minute she was wide awake because she heard her grandfather's voice shout, "Oh! I can't bear it. I can't." Then again she could hear many people crying. Aina ran to the room and she stood shocked. All the people of her immediate family were in the midst of hopeless sorrow. Her Daadi, her Baba, Prasad Baba, Rukmini Amma, and her parents were all weeping.

"Oh! Has someone died?" thought Aina with fear.

Daadi was saying, "But are you sure?"

Mahavir said, "Yes we are. I recognized her and so did Kalka. I knew that Prasad would be outside the palace, staging the protest demonstration. Kalka called Prasad inside and he also recognized her."

Suddenly Rukmini Amma spoke up loudly and angrily in a ranting voice, "You all are responsible. You all never listened to me even when I begged you to let her come back home. You all have made my darling daughter suffer such a horrible fate. Oh! My Sudha!"

Aina stood transfixed as she heard her Rukmini Amma's voice. It was shocking because her Rukmini Amma never spoke in front of her elders but just looked after them quietly. Now she was shouting at them and actually blaming them for Sudha. 'Sudha'! Aina did not remember any Sudha. Now she tried to piece the story from the disjointed sentences spoken by the elders.

Rukmini shouted, "Sudha was my daughter so no one was concerned for her. Only I, Sudha's mother have cried for Sudha. You others were always more angry than sad, when her name came up. And one day my husband actually declared that no one would take the name of Sudha in the house. Isn't this injustice? Aren't you all criminals?Give me an answer, you brutes."

When everyone was quiet, she shouted, "What wrong did my poor daughter do? Was she responsible that some ruffians had seen her and had decided to take her away? How brutal you all were! Those vile ruffians forced her. You could see that they were forcing her. They rubbed beef on her lips and you turned my poor daughter away. Away from her own house! Now why are you crying on seeing her at the Nawab's house and coming to know that Munni Bai is actually my daughter Sudha and that she has become a prostitute. Oh! It hurts me to think what a lot my poor child must have suffered. I want my daughter back, even if she is a prostitute."

"No," shouted all of them together.

"Yes. I will get her back whatever you all may say," shrieked Rukmini.

Her tears dried up as Prasad shouted, "How can we bring a prostitute home?"

Rukmini Amma shouted, "She became a prostitute because you all turned her out of the house. Now you have got a chance to repent and make up."

"She is already defiled. She cannot come here whatever you may say," said Prasad.

Rukmini said, "Again you are making a mistake by forsaking your own daughter. Why? Just because she is a woman? Just because she might have been used for the hunger of evil men? How is she to blame? Don't our family members go to prostitutes? You men are responsible for this. I will bring Sudha home to stay."

Even Daadi said, "No Rukmini. What will people say?"

"Let people go to hell. I don't care. The life of my daughter counts. Her sufferings must be so intense. Take me to my daughter. If you don't take me, then I will go to the Nawab's house myself."

"Have you gone mad? The whole city will resound with this news," said Prasad to his wife.

"I don't care," said Rukmini Amma.

"Keep quiet. Don't shout at each other. I will think of a way. Yes, I will invite Munni Bai for an evening here. Generally she dances only at the Nawab's house but he may allow her to come here," said her Baba.

"I am already here. I am Sudha," said a voice.

A woman dressed in rich clothes stood there in the outer doorway. Aina stared at the woman. Sudha! Beautiful she still was, but her suffering showed on her face. The tangible sorrow in her eyes gave her a pinched look. She stood decked up in finery, alone. Rukmini Amma ran towards Sudha but Prasad Baba caught her.

He rasped, "No. We shouldn't welcome a prostitute."

"Who made her a prostitute? You," said Rukmini.

Sudha said, "Father, I had not encouraged the ruffians in anyway. They saw me when there was an accident with my palanquin and I fell off. Thereupon the hooligans rubbed beef on my lips because they wanted to make me a prostitute. But at that time how could you throw me out of your house? Didn't you love me?"

Her father did not have an answer, but he said in a grating voice, "Why did you become a prostitute?"

"What could I have done? They forced me. They picked me up and took me to Benaras. There a man bought me for the Nawab of Anosi. I was helpless. Because you all had spurned me, I had nowhere to go. They would thrash me when I disobeyed them. So I accepted it as my fate. Why are you blaming me? If you had accepted me when they had rubbed beef on my lips, I would still be with you. Oh God! I would have been spared so many agonies. Why did you give me to those wolves? How do I become impure just by having beef rubbed on my face? A gram of meat spoilt my life and you all let it happen. Oh Ma, I have suffered so much," said Sudha as she burst out crying uncontrollably.

Rukmini Amma shouted, "Let me go to my daughter."

Prasad said, "No. She is a bad woman."

Rukmini shouted, "She is not bad. You are bad because you knowingly forsook your daughter. I feel like being with my daughter and now I am going to get what I want." She freed herself from his hold to run across to Sudha and hold her tight. The mother and daughter could not be separated how much the others tried.

But then Sudha said, "Mother. I have to go now."

"No," screamed her mother. "I will not let you go."

Sudha slowly disentangled herself from her mother and said, "I came here only because I saw Uncle and Father at the party at the Nawab's palace and saw them getting shocked and upset. I came as I was afraid something might happen to them. Let me go now."

Rukmini said, "You are thinking about them. What about the misery you are suffering Sudha?"

Sudha said, "It is my life. I am used to it now. I don't want to spoil the reputation of my family. I have come in a closed palanquin just now to keep my identity hidden. I know all the children have to be married. Aina has to be married. If the society comes to know that the prostitute Munni Bai is your daughter Sudha, these children will never get married. You are

Aina, aren't you? You were just a baby when I had to leave this house. I named you Aina. Come here child. Come to me."

The elders then realized that Aina was also standing in the room. Aina ran to her Aunt and was hugged with a fierce despairing love.

Both of them started crying and Aina said, "I will not let you go, Sudha."

"I am your aunt, your Bua," said Sudha.

"Bua don't go away," said Aina.

"Please Aina I can't stay here," said Sudha.

"You are sacrificing yourself again for these people? The same people who forsook you Sudha?" said Rukmini Amma.

"They are my family, Ma and I love them even if they do not love me. But Ma, please see that nothing like this happens to Aina," said Sudha.

Aina shouted angrily, "I won't let them spoil my life. I will make my own life. I will not listen to these hardhearted people. I will do what I want. Why would a woman be made a prostitute if the menfolk did not go there?" Everyone was quiet. Sudha patted Aina on her head and pulled away. She covered herself with a shawl, then she quietly walked out into the darkness.

Aina felt extremely upset. She turned round and shouted, "You all are butchers. I will not let you spoil my life like you spoilt my aunt's life. Rukmini Amma is right. You have done a very bad thing by not accepting Sudha Bua. You have made her suffer. I will not obey you all."

From that day, things were not the same again for Aina. Aina refused to talk to any one in the family, except her mother and Rukmini Amma. Gone were the days of the past unfolding in her Baba's stories. Now he too seemed a villain who played with the lives of women.

One day she told her mother, "I want to study a lot. I want to earn money. I want to be independent."

"But no one in the whole family will let you be independent, so why are you rebelling against norms?"

"Ma if Sudha bua had been educated then she could have run away from the Nawab and learnt to live alone. If she could have earned money, she could have been independent. These men earn money and so they think that they are God's own creation."

"We women cannot show our faces to men."

Aina replied, "Sabal chacha told me that there are schools where only girls study. Send me there. Sabal chacha told me that in the big cities women are getting educated and are earning a lot of money, but here we are following traditions of the ancient past."

"We have to follow traditions."

"Why? Why do we let ourselves get stuck in a pigeon hole just because men order us about? We should follow only what is good. Women can earn good money too. These men know that. So they don't let us go out. They are afraid that we won't need them. I hate men. I won't care for any man. I will only use men. I will play with them as they play with the lives of so many women. But first I have to be independent. I will go out of the house. I will study. I will break the restrictions."

Her mother shouted, "Don't you dare talk like that! You must not become rebellious."

"I was only expressing my opinion," said Aina.

Gomti said, "You are not supposed to have an opinion. A woman needs to sacrifice."

"Ma, men don't make sacrifices, why should we?"

"Stop it. This is what you should not speak. You have to obey the elders. You have to respect the norms of society. Promise me that you will always be ready to adjust, for my sake. You keep your hand on my head and swear that you will always do the right thing that doesn't bring ill repute to our family's name, otherwise you will see my dead face," said her mother.

Gomti pulled Aina's hand onto her own head and Aina said, "All right Ma, I promise but only on the condition that you send me to school. Do you remember that Swami Ram said that I will suffer? I want to be ready to face life, and education is very important. This you will have to do for me if you want me to obey you. Will you?"

CHAPTER 15

So Aina went to school, but only after a little more psychological arm twisting of her family members. She just stopped eating till they agreed to send her to school. True that at first Daadi would not let her go to the missionary Convent school because the girls there had to wear skirts. "How shameless! Their legs will be visible. No, Aina can't go to this school." But Baba talked to the Principal and got special permission for Aina to wear a long trouser-like shalwar under the uniform skirt, then Aina was allowed to go to the best English medium Convent school in Najapur. Before she went to school, Veena Amma came and blessed Aina and talked to her alone. This was very unusual.

Veena was the widow of the youngest brother of Mahavir and Prasad, who had died on their wedding night. Veena Amma, lived in the farthest room of the palace because she was not allowed to mix up with the others. That is why, even for Aina, Veena was just a distant relative. Like every widow, she also was considered inauspicious by everyone, except by Rukmini and Gomti. So Veena liked the two of them, but the callous attitude of her other in-laws hurt her so much, that she herself chose not to meet the other family members, except when totally unavoidable.

Veena said, "I am so glad Aina that you are going to study in a school. All the best."

Aina loved her school which opened up a new world for Aina which at times overwhelmed her. Books helped her. She loved reading because the story books opened up a world of fantasy, far removed from her inhibited and cloistered existence at home. She took time to bring a balance in her mind between the two.

She studied hard to become a good student because she really enjoyed studies. Somehow she felt that studies would be her ticket to freedom. With a passion and focus she studied. She did very well in her exams. It was touching for her to see the happiness in the eyes of her Baba when she came first in class. Her Baba rewarded her with a princely sum of 21 rupees.

Then she fought again with all the family members. Now she wanted that all the girls in the family should study. Slowly the elders had to relent. Now all the girls of the family were finally being educated because of Aina, and Veena Amma was the happiest about this.

Now the girls had more freedom. They could come in open 'rickshaws' without covering their heads. Moreover they could go in skirts because Daadi relented too after going to Aina's school for the PT display, when Aina tripped because of the loose pant and lost a race.

Then one night, Sudha came to their house, while all the menfolk had gone to another feast. Sudha came in a closed palanquin and stayed till late in the night. Aina went to Daadi and persuaded and convinced her to come and sit with Sudha. Daadi also accepted Sudha and sat with her for sometime, but the rest of the womenfolk refused to welcome her. Rukmini Amma went to make dinner as she wanted to cook all the favourite dishes for her poor daughter Sudha.

Aina said, "Sudha Bua. You must have suffered a lot."

"My life has been traumatic and I was not bold enough like you," said Sudha.

"Are you a virgin, Sudha Bua?" said Aina.

"What a funny question to ask a prostitute, but yes, I am," said Sudha.

"Then why does everyone call you a bad woman?" asked Aina.

Sudha said, "They don't know the truth. They think that the Nawab is normal. Actually he is quite a fool and he has no inclination towards sex. He keeps me as a prostitute just to maintain the façade that he is virile and has a high status, and that suits me. I am like a trophy that he loves to flaunt in front of others. In a way I am happy with it, because I hate anyone touching me."

"I also don't like men touching me. Don't you go to other men, Sudha Bua?" asked Aina.

"No. I am the Nawab's keep. He does not send me anywhere else," said Sudha.

"Are you happy, Bua?" asked Aina.

"I have money given by the Nawab and a lot of jewels and he has even given the house to me. The only problem is my reputation," said Sudha.

"Bua, I asked if you are happy," repeated Aina.

Sudha sighed and tears fell unchecked down her cheeks, "Happiness? I am a woman and women are not supposed to even think of happiness. Our life and destiny are dotted with tears."

"What do you regret the most?" asked Aina.

"Not having children. I wish I had children, Aina," said Sudha. There was an ache in her voice. "On second thoughts though, I am happy as I am. My child would have had to bear the stigma of being illegitimate and would have been called the child of a prostitute."

It hurt Aina and she said, "Women accept so much pain. Why don't you rebel? I will never allow a man to trouble me so much and Baba says that there should be no tears ever."

Sudha said, "Aina I can't. I am now in this filth and cannot get out of it. I hope you can do what you want, but my child, be prepared for pain, because these men cut up the very souls of us women."

Aina's mother Gomti came and sat down with Sudha. Then Gomti said, "I am worried about Aina. We have not got any good match for her. Recently a common friend hinted on a proposal from a Rai family. Have you heard about them? They were two brothers and only one of them had a son Daman Rai, who is the heir. Though he is a bit old, he is an eligible match. Should I give a proposal for Aina?"

Aina shouted, "Ma, I don't want to get married."

Gomti said, "I am not asking you Aina. Shut up. Girls do not interfere with the talks about their marriage. You will do as we say. It is a matter of shame that we haven't been able to marry you by now, but now we are not as rich as we used to be. Sudha, tell me."

"Are you talking about the Rai family of Rojpur?" asked Sudha.

"Yes. They are very wealthy people," said Gomti.

"They are very strange people," said Sudha.

"What do you mean Sudha?" asked Gomti.

"Actually the father and uncle of Daman Rai were not normal. These two brothers could not sire a child. The elder brother was impotent. The younger brother was frigid. He abhorred sex and so he stayed away from women. So naturally their wives could not give them an heir."

"How do you know?" asked Aina.

Gomti said, "Aina. Go away from here."

"Let her be here. Girls should be innocent, but not ignorant. The Nawab has an eunuch Laila. He was friendly with the elder brother's servant. He told Laila and Laila told me."

"Oh! Do you think that proposal will not be good? What will I do now?" said Gomti.

"Leave her alone, and let her study," said Sudha.

Gomti said, "Don't fill her head with all this nonsense."

Sudha sent Aina to get a glass of water but Aina waited outside the door because she understood that Sudha had sent her away on purpose. Sure enough, Aina heard Sudha say to Gomti, "It is said that Daman is not the child of either of these two brothers. They called someone to impregnate the elder one's wife Ram Katori, then she conceived and delivered Daman. She is the only one who survives today. The other wife and the two brothers of the family are already dead."

Suddenly someone put a hand on Aina's shoulder and she screamed. A voice said, "Aina. What are you doing out here?" It was Rukmini Amma and Gomti scolded Aina for listening behind the door.

Aina came and sat down again and thankfully everyone forgot about her. She was left alone again with Sudha after some time and she kept on asking Sudha about her life. Soon food was served and Sudha had her favourite dishes. "Do you cook? How is the Nawab's palace?" asked Aina.

"Very grand. The Nawab lives in a huge palace with his wives. I live separately in a small palace. He has given the palace to me. I have servants so I don't have to cook," said Sudha.

"How lucky!" said Aina and then she bit her tongue because Sudha burst out crying.

"I am not lucky Aina. I am a prostitute. I am an outcaste from society. See only you, your mother and your Rukmini Amma are here. Even your Daadi did not want to eat with me. All the womenfolk have not come here even to meet me," sobbed Sudha.

"But I have come to meet you," said a voice. They all looked up to see Veena standing there.

Sudha leapt up and embraced Veena saying, "Veena Chachi. How nice of you. How are you?"

"Aina was right. You are lucky Sudha. Atleast you don't have to suffer loneliness like me. I suffer it, though I am in the midst of such a huge family," said Veena. They talked for some time. They suddenly heard some voices and Rukmini Amma said, "Sudha. The menfolk have come. Go back."

Sudha got up and ran to the back door. Her closed palanquin was standing behind. She quickly sat in it and was taken away. The women looked at the anger on the men's faces and quaked.

CHAPTER 16

The men had seen the closed palanquin and understood that Sudha had come. But the women were spared punishment because as soon as Sudha went away, one aunt came running, shouting, "Bela is in labour. Come quickly. She has a complication."

Some youngsters were sent to call the midwife. She came hurrying and took charge of the situation, going to Bela at once. Bela was the wife of Hari, an elder cousin of Aina. Everyone got out of their beds and tried to help in some way. Aina thought how different it was on this day to what had been in the past when some years back Hari had married Bela.

It was a love marriage. There had been such an uproar in the family. Hari and Bela had been turned out. But after the intervention of Rukmini Amma, Hari and Bela had been called back and accepted by the whole family. Today the whole family was worried for Bela who was a very sweet girl. She really looked after the elders.

All of a sudden Rukmini came and stood before Bela's mother-in-law Laxmi and said, "The midwife says that there is some complication. Maybe both the mother and child may not survive. She can assure that she can save one. Whom do you want saved, Bela or the child?"

Laxmi said, "Save the child."

However Hari shouted, "No. Tell the midwife to save my wife Bela."

Finally Daadi and Mahavir decided that the midwife should try and save Bela.

Aina felt stark terror inside her. She stood outside nervously biting her nails. Soon a child's cry drowned the silence but nobody even muttered anything. Then Rukmini's voice could be heard, "Both Bela and the child are safe. The child is a son. Congratulations."

The whole family was ecstatic about it. The midwife was given a generous reward by Daadi.

After that, life went on for Aina with her studies and playing with Bela's child at home. After a few months, the barber was called. There was a feast planned to be given to celebrate the ceremony of the 'mundan' in which the child's hair would be shaved from his scalp. Ma went to the barber and asked, "What happened about the marriage proposal of Aina?"

The barber said, "Unfortunately the first party wants a fair complexioned girl. The second party is asking for a lot of dowry, much more than you can give."

Gomti saw Aina standing with Rukmini Amma and she said to Aina, "I wish I could get you married, but it is proving so difficult to get a match for you. If only you were not a daughter but a son!"

Aina felt very hurt. That day, while the family rejoiced, Aina went and sat alone on the terrace, the first time not afraid of being alone. For the first time she liked the peace and quiet, but felt an irritation at the regular festivities in the house, despite paucity of funds.

Soon the eunuchs came. There was one elderly eunuch whom everyone called Basanti and she had a group of younger eunuchs, all wearing female attire and flashy dresses. Parwati made them sing and dance for a long time and the whole family watched them. Basanti started teasing Aina's mother Gomti the most.

Gomti looked quite perturbed, but she said nothing. Aina thought that it was strange that women could come out in front of eunuchs, but not in front of men. On second thoughts, she realized that it wasn't strange. Women were not safe with men because of their libido. Atleast the women were safe with eunuchs.

When the eunuchs had finished dancing and singing, Daadi gave them a lot of money. The eunuchs were very happy and blessed the newborn child.

Aina asked Daadi, "Why did you give so much money to them?"

"We should always try and get the blessings of eunuchs. Moreover Basanti has been coming to our house since long. How could I have sent her back empty handed?" asked Daadi.

That night they had a feast to celebrate. Three dancing girls had also been called and all the members of the family sat down in the huge hall. Everyone was drinking, and boisterous merriment chuckled through their huge house, more so because Prasad was not there. Mahavir had been sick for a fortnight, but he came out and sat down with a glass of rum to see the dance.

The dancing girls sang and danced. The men of the family sat in the front. One dancing girl Moti bai was quite fair and not very slim, but she danced very well, though she didn't look very young. She had never come to their house before. She started singing and dancing. She had anklet bells on her feet and Aina was simply mesmerized by the grace and beauty of her agile dance movements despite her age.

The two other nautch girls would continue dancing, flirting with all the men, but Moti Bai focused on Mahavir. It seemed as if she sang just for Mahavir and no one else. Inside all the women were watching the dance, without being seen themselves, as women were still not allowed the freedom to come out and meet strangers. Raju had come from Lucknow and now he became drunk and he started flirting with Moti bai, who looked at Mahavir as if imploring him to control Raju.

Rukmini saw the look and whispered, "Is she the prostitute where he goes?"

Aina understood that Rukmini was talking of her Baba keeping Moti Bai as a mistress. All the women started looking at Moti bai with interest as Mahavir reacted strongly. He shouted at Raju and told him to get out. Raju was forced to go from there. Raju went away ranting at Mahavir, but then on the signal of Mahavir, Moti bai resumed singing and dancing. Just then their security guard came running in, shouting, "Many people have barged inside the front courtyard."

The noise of slogans suddenly rent the air. Kalka saw that Prasad had come with the people of his organisation. They were all holding black flags and were shouting slogans to stop the dancing.

Mahavir said, "Do as they say." Kalka asked the dancing girls to leave and Mahavir saw to it that they left safely by the back door, so that they would not be troubled by the protestors outside in the front of the palace. Before going Moti bai came to Mahavir.

Moti bai didn't see Aina standing behind Mahavir and she asked him, "How are you feeling now? It has been a fortnight since you came."

"I am better now. Take care of yourself. I will definitely come next week," said Mahavir.

On hearing this, somehow Aina felt let down because it was confirmed that her Baba used to go to Moti bai's house. Aina felt pity for her Daadi. As the nautch girls walked off, the festivities ended, but the spirit of the women at home bubbled and could not be subdued. They started singing and dancing.

The men sitting outside could not see them dance, but they could hear their voices. The men also enjoyed listening to their songs. Suddenly Mahavir got up and said, "I think we men are denying ourselves by staying here while the ladies are in purdah. Come on folks, we must put an end to this purdah system."

All the male members got up and walked into the inner courtyard. Daadi was scandalized. Most of the women pulled down their veils to a longer length, but Mahavir said, "Ladies, we have come to hear you sing. From today, purdah is totally banished from our house." All the men sat down on the floor and then the women sang. Mahavir also asked the girls to dance. When Aina danced then Mahavir gave her five rupees as a reward and said, "I had no idea you could dance so well Aina."

Everyone was enjoying when Prasad came back in the night. He was relieved to see that the atmosphere at home was still one of festivity. No one had any grudge against Prasad either. He realized that all the men were sitting with the ladies in the inner court, but he did not comment on it. He also joined them. He was welcomed cheerfully as they all sat down for dinner.

Aina had noticed that Veena had not taken part in the festivities. She realized that Veena actually kept away from all the celebrations always. She felt sorry for her.

She felt guilty that she had never bothered about the lonely Veena. Aina now made up her mind to be kind to her. She started spending time with Veena.

Veena had a lot of restrictions put on her just because she was a widow. She was considered to be inauspicious and she was not allowed to attend any celebration. Aina talked to her Daadi and asked her to stop the restrictions on Veena but in vain.

CHAPTER 17

The next night, Aina couldn't sleep. She tossed and turned restlessly. Suddenly she froze. She had heard a click. It was the door leading to the back lane. Was it a robber? She felt paralysed with fear.

She knew that the sound was coming from the room of her parents. Now the norms of her family had been changed and rooms had been given to all the couples, so that a husband and his wife could live together. Again Aina heard a hushed sound and panic gripped her. Someone was definitely there.

Aina was just forcing the frightened muscles of her rigid mouth to shout, "Help! Thief!" when she heard a voice whispering, "Why have you come here? Quick, go outside or someone will see you." It was her mother's voice. Aina was shocked to hear her mother's voice.

Another voice said, "I had to come." The voice was very hoarse. Aina got up softly and peeped at the back lane through her door. Her mother was standing outside on the steps leading to the back lane from her room. Another fat person was standing out in the lane. Their furtive voices reached Aina's window where her curious ears heard each word.

Her Ma said, "Why have you come?"

"I am dying. I am very sick. I need money," said the hoarse voice.

"But I don't have money," said her Ma.

"See I helped you once. Now you must help me."

"I know. But I have no money. What can I do?"

"This necklace. You can give it to me. I will sell it and get medicines," said the hoarse voice.

"How will I explain it to everyone?" asked Ma.

"You have a choice. Either you explain to them or I explain what happened to your son," said the hoarse voice, now more rough and threatening than before.

"No. You promised that you will never tell," said Ma.

The hoarse voice said, "You are a strange woman. I came so many times to your house. Did you never want to know where he is?"

Her mother replied, "No. I don't want to know."

"All right. Give me the necklace and I will go away."

Aina was shocked to see her mother take off her necklace and give it to the person with the hoarse voice. Then Ma whispered, "Now go quickly."

As the person started moving away slowly, Aina heard her Ma say in a small voice, "Where is he?"

The person stopped and the hoarse voice said, "At the Nawab's palace."

"What! What is his name?" gasped Ma.

"Give me your gold bangles and then I will tell you his name," said the voice.

"No. I don't want to hear. Go away," said Ma and she rushed in and closed the door. Then Aina heard her crying her heart out.

Aina thought, "That means that father hasn't come back yet from Bijli's house or Ma would be totally quiet. She wouldn't cry in front of him."

Aina lay down but she could not sleep. Who was this person? He had talked of her mother's son. That means, my brother. But I have Munna, my brother. Why would Ma give a necklace because of Munna? And Munna is at home. He was not in the Nawab's palace. It was all very strange. But Aina then got an answer to another thought of hers. She had felt that the hoarse voice and the fat person were somehow familiar. The voice was masculine but the figure was wearing a sari. Now she recollected who that person was.

The person was the eunuch Basanti.

Aina wasn't aware when she slept, but the next day she woke up with an ominous feeling, as if something bad was going to happen. Aina knew what she had been worried about, when Daadi looked at her mother and shouted, "Where is your necklace?"

"I must have lost it," said her Ma.

"You lose a lot of jewellery. This is bad," said Daadi.

Her Ma kept quiet and everyone started finding the necklace, but it was nowhere to be found.

Just then they heard the voice of Kalka saying, "Ma. Girish has come. He has got a better job. He is earning very well now." They started congratulating each other and Prasad. Though Girish was Prasad's elder son by his first wife, still Rukmini loved Girish as her own son. The elders declared that they would celebrate.

In the preparations for the party to celebrate the job that Girish had got, everyone soon forgot about the necklace and Aina heaved a sigh of relief. She realized that she had been very tense about what her mother would do about the necklace she had given to Basanti.

In that party, the men and women of the family celebrated together. The women still had their faces covered though. Everyone danced and sang because, on the orders of Mahavir, no dancing girls were called.

Then Aina saw that glasses of a drink were being given to everyone and special sweetmeats which the women had been preparing, were being served. From a corner of the open courtyard, Aina saw Rukmini Amma going into a room. Rukmini called Aina and said, "We are putting 'bhang' (opium) in the drink. See that the children don't drink this as it is an intoxicant."

Later, that night was remembered always with convulsive laughter, as it turned out to be quite a weird experience. All the adults became intoxicated. When one person cried, all of them would cry. When one person sang, all of them would sing. When another person laughed, then all of them would laugh. Aina watched the intoxicated family members making fools of themselves.

The worst hit was her Prasad Baba. He was unaware that he was having bhang, so he had two glasses. Rukmini made him eat a lot of sweets which enhanced the effect of the bhang. Then Prasad started giving a lecture to his elder brother Mahavir.

After that both of them started dancing. It was hilarious to see the stern Prasad sing and dance. Rukmini enjoyed it the most. Finally everyone slept.

The next morning saw the family members nursing hangovers, and fiery were the scoldings given to the culprits who had planned this prank.

The next morning also made it clear that money, or rather the scarcity of money had become a big issue for the family. Girish had already gone back to Lucknow, so when the bills had to be paid for the party of the previous night, as well as the monthly ration, there was no money in the house to pay them. It seemed that they would again have to take a loan to pay up the bills.

The discussion heated up when Daadi said, "We need to have money. Let me tell you that it is becoming very difficult to run the house. Now the earning members of the family don't contribute money to the house kitty."

Aina stood in a corner and listened to all this. She had realized that their financial position was pathetic. The 'Zamindari Act' had seen to it that Mahavir did not get any more income from the villages in his name. Slowly the farmers had taken over his land. There was no other income but the expenses were the same. Celebrations were always done in style even if loans had to be taken. And the piling debts had started hurting the happiness of the family. Aina did not like it.

She spoke up, "Why do we have so many celebrations if we don't have the money? If we had saved the ten thousand rupees given by the Nawab, we would not have been in this position."

Daadi shouted, "Aina, why do you always listen to the talk of elders? Go away and play."

Prasad said, "Aina is saying the right thing. We should cut extra expenses. We do waste money."

"Prasad is right Parwati. We should cut costs and live within our means because our income has been completely depleted. Then the young men of our family are leaving the house and going to other cities for their jobs, but it is so expensive in the cities that they cannot send us money," said Mahavir.

Subsequently the celebrations lessened, but the money position had an impact on Aina. She realized how miserable the lack of money could make a family and she hated it that her happy family was slowly being reduced to many irritated members snapping at each other with animosity.

Mahavir said one day, "I think that I should take up a job."

"At your age you should rest. You have worked enough," said Parwati.

Aina knew that Prasad had already started looking for a job. Till now he had not done any job in his life because he had spent time in taking out processions against social evils. He finally got an accountant's job with a lawyer but the money was enough only for his immediate family.

Girish had a better job but he had to support Sabal in starting his law practice, and also Prabal who wanted to study more. Kalka also started thinking of sending Munna for higher studies to the city.

Daadi insisted that Munna should be married off early and then sent outside, but Mahavir and Prasad decided that the wedding of Munna should be after Munna had started earning for himself.

Finally it was decided that after the Holi festival, Munna would go to the city for his holidays. In the city, Munna would stay in the same house where Sabal and Prabal and the other boys were staying with Girish. He would try for admission but education was costly. This additional cost would prove very difficult for the family. The talks of the family now always veered around money. Aina hated the pinch of money and she said to Mahavir, "Baba. I think we should have a lot of money otherwise one feels so miserable. You should marry me to a man who is very rich. I don't want to face this misery in my life. I should have enough money to splurge."

"Even if the boy you get married to is twenty years older than you?" asked Baba laughingly.

"No. Twenty years is a bit old. But get me a rich husband," said Aina, with her eyes full of laughter.

"Oh my God, this shameless girl is talking to her grandfather about her own marriage. When will you learn to be like a girl?" asked Daadi.

"Never," exclaimed Aina and went off laughing.

Mahavir looked at her with love in his eyes and said wistfully, "I hope that Aina gets a very good match and is very happy in her life. We must try more for getting a good bridegroom for her."

But instead of Aina, the topic of Munna's wedding heated up. The barber came to finalise the dowry to be taken for Munna's wedding. The barber was sent away and the discussions started.

Prasad spoke up, "Dowry is a wrong thing. We should not take dowry. I am protesting with my group against this practice. I will take a procession holding black flags even tomorrow to a wedding where dowry has been asked for and given. How can I tolerate this happening in my own house?"

Daadi said, "How will we then get enough money to give dowry for Aina? How will we manage the wedding expenses of Girish, Sabal and Prabal? That is why we have to take dowry for Munna."

And no one could shake her from her stance. One day when Prasad was not present, the rest of the people discussed the amount to be taken as dowry and this was conveyed through the barber to Sonali's parents. After some days, the barber came again.

Sonali's father had agreed to the dowry but they had requested if the wedding could take place earlier, because Sonali's grandmother was sick and dying.

The answer could only be 'Yes'. Hurriedly the preparations were done for an early wedding of Sonali and Munna. After the wedding rituals, Sonali was to stay with her parents till Munna finished his studies. Munna had seen his bride and she was beautiful. That made him very happy. After that Munna went again to the city to study. He stayed with Girish in Lucknow.

Gomti cried for a long time when Munna was about to go, but Munna was not overly perturbed. He was looking forward to enjoying life in Lucknow. He left without a backward glance at his mother, who on the other hand, cried copiously for days. Sonali's family had given a nice dowry of thirty thousand rupees which was a lot of money. Everyone was thrilled as now they had money to give to Aina for her dowry.

So Gomti shifted her attention and focused it on getting Aina married. Many people started coming to 'see' Aina. In the past days, the barber and his wife would get a marriage settled, but now the parents of the boy would come to 'see' the girl themselves. Though Aina understood that this was essential, she was very embarrassed by this. She had to carry a tea tray with snacks and show herself to the boy's parents. She did it just because her mother ordered her, but when one after another, she faced rejections, she started hating the whole system of showing a girl to the groom's family.

CHAPTER 18

One day her mother said, "Get ready Aina because a family is coming to see you."

"Am I a cow that they are going to buy? Why should I show myself? I hate it," screamed Aina, but in the end she was forced to get ready in a sari. Again she was rejected because she was not fair. Aina stood in front of the mirror and looked at herself.

Her Ma came in and said, "Aina. Put milk cream on your face then rub it off. Then you will look fairer."

"Ma I am happy as I am. I never thought that I was bad looking," said Aina seriously.

"No Aina you are not bad looking. You have sharp features and you are attractive, but people look for beauty in girls and for them fair is beautiful. For me you are beautiful as you are," said Gomti.

This was the first time that her mother had said something nice about her. Aina knew that her mother was focusing on her because Munna had gone away. Aina felt bad that her mother thought of her only because Munna was not there. Still the pain in her heart subsided a bit and Aina ran to her mother and held her. Then she cried and cried. When she could talk she said, "I am sorry Ma that you are having trouble marrying me off. I wish for your sake that I was fairer."

"You don't have to be sorry, Aina. Those people don't know what they are missing. And now what happened about your resolve not to shed tears?"

Aina said, "Because these rejections have hurt me."

Aina was thinking how she loved her mother in this good and playful mood. She had never seen her mother so happy before. And then her mother said, "Aina write a letter to Munna from my side." Now Aina understood. Her mother had received a letter from Munna from Lucknow. The letter had asked for more money, yet Gomti was happy that Munna's letter had come. Gomti could not read the letter because she was illiterate, that is why she had been loving towards Aina.

They spent some time writing the letter from Gomti's side to Munna. Aina felt jealous as she heard the loving words that Gomti wanted to write to Munna. After finishing the letter, her mother said, "Why are you looking depressed? Come on snap out of it. We have to prepare for the 'Holi' festival which is coming soon. Munna will come for Holi. I am waiting for him."

Some nights before Holi, they were having dinner, when they heard someone banging on the front gate. They ran to find out what was happening. Some miscreants were trying to break their gate.

Hari was the first one to reach. He shouted, "What are you doing?"

"We are taking wood for burning Holika," said one of the miscreants.

Before Holi every year, a bonfire was burnt at the main crossing of every neighbourhood. These drunk miscreants were taking their front wooden gate to burn in the bonfire being stacked on the crossroads near their house. Hari slapped them and sent the three miscreants away. After half an hour while they were having dinner, there was a commotion again and they saw that those men had come back. Hari dashed outside angrily, but then he saw that many men were standing outside with bamboos, sticks and knives. It was too late for Hari to escape and the miscreants started hitting Hari.

The family realized too late that the three miscreants had brought their gang of ruffians who were hitting Hari with great cruelty and finally he was stabbed. When all the members of the house ran out, the miscreants ran away, leaving a grieving family behind, because Hari had died in Bela's arms. Their Holi had become totally without colour. There was deep mourning, but when the elder women started saying that Bela should be given the lonely life that Veena had suffered as a widow, Veena came forward.

She said, "No. Bela will live a normal life. No one should tell her she is inauspicious. No one should segregate her from the family. No one should force her to wear rough cotton clothes. No one should coerce her to eat bland food.No one should banish her from society. If you all trouble her, I will call the police."

Rukmini and Gomti supported Veena, and Bela was not made to suffer what Veena had suffered on becoming a widow. This gave immense satisfaction to Veena. But the next day Bela was not in the house. Her mother-in-law Laxmi went looking for her, asking all the members of the family where Bela could be. Everyone was perturbed at the disappearance of Bela.

Daadi said, "Where could Bela go? Is she so hardhearted that she cannot mourn for her husband Hari even for the stipulated thirteen days?"

Aina said, "How can you say a thing like this Daadi? Why are you ready to believe the worst about everyone? She may have had a good reason to go."

"You have become a real granny. Don't you dare talk to me like this," Daadi was really angry, her nose absolutely red. Just then Bela came back and her mother-in-law Laxmi expended her anger on her.

Laxmi ranted at Bela, "I was always against your marriage. See how right I was. Where were you till now? Widows are supposed to mourn their dead husband."

Bela listened to her tirade and then said, "Ma. I am mourning him. My grief is so great that I don't want to think about it, because if I think then I will go mad and that I cannot afford just now, because I have to look after all of us and I have to earn money for ourselves."

"You don't have to earn money. I won't allow you to go out of the house," shouted Laxmi.

"Then Ma, how will we manage?" asked Bela.

"This is the insurance that a joint family gives us," said Laxmi.

"Ma, even a joint family needs money. Hari used to earn money for us. We gave our contribution to Daadi and the rest we kept for the essential expenses of our family. Do you want to become a burden on Daadi? I don't. So I talked to Hari's boss. He has given me a job."

Laxmi screeched, "Will a daughter-in-law of this great house go out and work?"

Bela said, "Yes. I have to, otherwise how will we survive? I refuse to stay on other people's charity. And till when can anyone fend for a complete family? Ma you don't have any other son. I am your son from today. I need to earn for your three daughters yet to be married."

"What will people say?" asked Laxmi.

Bela said, "What people are you talking about? Will these people give us money to manage? If they say anything, send them to me and I will answer them."

Laxmi became quiet, feeling a grudging respect for her courageous daughter-in-law and Bela started working and no one criticized her. Rather she was praised for being so strong.

Daadi said, "How things change. I never stepped out of my house, but now our daughters-in-law are going out to do jobs. I am sure society will laugh at us."

Baba said, "We should move with the times and when this so-called society says anything, tell it to keep quiet. You say that you have given permission to Bela to work, as there is no difference between girls and boys."

Daadi started chanting God's name. She distracted herself by thinking of Aina's marriage, but as Hari had died, they could not celebrate Holi ever again and they could not have any auspicious occasion for a full year, so Aina's marriage would have to wait again. Life was sober and sad after this incident, as no one could forget the cheerful Hari who had been quite a favourite with everyone. All of them went through the routine of life mechanically without zest.

After the stipulated time of a year, her Ma again started talking about getting Aina married.

Aina told her grandmother one day, "Daadi. I don't want to be married early. So please tell Ma to stop showing me to people. I want to take a degree and be financially independent. Daadi, Bela has come from a big city. She is educated and so today she can look after her family. I also want to be like her."

"Shut up, you have to get married. The Rai family has sent a proposal for you again. See how lucky you are," said Daadi.

"There must be something wrong with them that they are sending proposals again and again, even though we don't reply in the affirmative," said Aina.

"What wrong can there be? I think you should be married there, because they are wealthy people and they are not asking for a dowry," said Daadi.

"I want to study further," said Aina stubbornly.

Daadi said, "See Aina. They are not asking for dowry. So we can give the money we got from Sonali's house to pay off some of our debts."

Then her Baba said, "Aina. We are becoming old. How long do you think we will live? Give us the pleasure of seeing your wedding. I know he is fifteen years older than you but he is wealthy and you wanted a wealthy husband. Say yes to this proposal."

Aina did not have the heart to refuse. She just nodded her head. That night she had a nightmare and she ran to her mother's room. She stood still as she heard her mother sniffling. Her mother was crying again. Aina was sure that she was crying, though her mother had covered her face.

Aina said, "Ma. You are crying for your son, isn't it?"

"Aina, why should I cry for Munna?"

Aina answered, "Not Munna. Another son. The one at the Nawab's palace."

Her Ma became very pale. She gasped, "How do you know?"

"That night I heard you. It was the eunuch Basanti who had come that day, wasn't it?"

"Yes," whispered her mother. "Did you hear everything?"

"Everything that was spoken by you both. But then you didn't ask the name of my brother, Ma. What is this secret of yours? Tell me. I may be of help to you."

Ma said, "I had another child, a son. But he was not normal. He was born an eunuch. I was then at my mother's house. Then a group of eunuchs came to celebrate the birth of this child. The old eunuch Basanti recognized me as he used to come here to our house. I gave my son to him."

"That is why you lose a lot of jewellery Ma, isn't it?" asked Aina.

"Yes, what can I do? Basanti always asks me for money. I never have money because your father does not earn anything. So I have to give my jewellery."

"Don't you want to meet your son?" asked Aina.

Gomti's face mirrored her doubts. "I feel strange. I am confused. On the one hand I want to meet him, but then I think I can't bear to see an eunuch as my son."

Aina said, "But it could be that my brother is the one who is friendly with Sudha Bua?"

"I have thought of this also," said Ma.

"Shouldn't we ask Sudha Bua?" asked Aina.

"No. I don't want anyone to know this secret. Promise me you will tell no one," said Ma.

Aina said firmly, "No I don't promise Ma. Just in case he needs our help, then I will be the first person to help him, but till then I will not tell anyone."

"Thank you," whispered Ma.

Aina hugged her close and said, "Ma. You did nothing wrong. You gave him a life. Maybe he is happy. You stop worrying yourself to death."

Suddenly there was a knock at the back door. Her mother stiffened and Aina said, "Relax Ma."

"It could be Basanti," said Ma.

"It could be Sudha bua," said Aina.

Aina looked outside from the window first and saw that it was Sudha. She went and opened the door. Sudha asked, "Are the men at home?"

"Yes," said Gomti.

"Then I will not come in. Can you call Ma?" asked Sudha.

Gomti said, "I will go and call Rukmini. Wait here in my room, Sudha."

Sudha whispered, "All right. Please hurry up." Sudha sat in Gomti's room. Gomti went inside to call Rukmini, and Aina told Sudha about how money was becoming a problem for the family.

Sudha said, "Money is a problem everywhere. Even the Nawab has financial problems. His youngest wife is claiming all the property. The court has frozen his accounts and assets."

CHAPTER 19

Aina also told Sudha about her eunuch brother who was working for the Nawab.

Sudha answered, "Only Laila is working there. It must be Laila who is your brother. Come to think of it, he resembles your mother. He has the same big eyes and fair complexion. Don't worry, I will keep this a secret and I will get Laila to come here to meet your mother."

Just then Rukmini came and hugged Sudha. Then Aina had no chance to talk to Sudha, as she talked with Rukmini and then went away in a hurry.

After two days Sudha knocked again at the backdoor in the middle of the night. As soon as Aina opened the back door, she saw Sudha standing with a young eunuch. Laila, her brother. Aina's heart started thumping painfully. Sudha saw Aina staring at Laila and said, "I have told him everything."

Aina walked ahead to embrace him, but Laila just put his hand on her head as Sudha said, "Laila. She is your sister Aina." The brother and sister looked at each other for a long time but could say nothing. There were tears in the eyes of Laila that spoke out all the misery and frustration of his life. When he looked around the room, Aina felt as if he was thinking of what might have been, if he had been normal and not been sent away. Then tears slid down Aina's cheeks but she wiped them away and led Laila to her mother.

Her mother was sleeping. She was woken up and then she stared at Laila. Sudha said gently, "He is your son." But it seemed as if Aina's mother had lost all her ability to move. She just stared at Laila and kept quiet. Laila came slowly and touched her feet and her mother put her hand on his head. But still both the mother and son seemed incapable of words.

Aina then saw a look on her mother's face. Was it a look despising what she had created in her own womb? Was it disgust? Was it loathing? Was it utter revulsion? It was certainly not a welcoming look of love. Laila also moved back and said to Sudha, "I want to go."

Sudha said, "Laila. This is your house. Would you like to stay in this house?"

Laila said brusquely, "No, I don't want to. I won't fit in. Why should I embarrass everyone? Let us go."

Sudha quietly took Laila away in her closed palanquin. Aina saw her mother sitting with a guilty look on her face. Aina had expected a happy reunion of mother and son and frankly, she was thoroughly disappointed. She in a way blamed her mother for not welcoming Laila with more love. She realized that she again felt let down by her mother, because her mother could only love Munna. She could not love Aina in the same way, and she had not been able to love Laila also.

But she now heard her mother's whisper, "I cannot accept him as my son. He looks so strange. Oh! He has my eyes but, he cannot be my son. I could not have produced such a freak of Nature. Oh! Why didn't I let him be killed? Why did I save him? He was looking at me in such a manner that I felt guilty."

Her mother was so emotionally upset that she couldn't even cry. She sat wide eyed looking at the place where Laila had been standing. Aina caressed her hair and made her lie down. She hated to see her mother looking so vulnerable and she was afraid that something might happen to Gomti. Then she said, "Ma relax. I called him because I wanted you to meet your son."

"But I feel so strange. There is something wrong with me. I should have been so happy meeting him, but I was actually ashamed of having given birth to him. I am bad," said Gomti.

Aina had thought the same thing and she felt guilty about thinking negatively about her mother. Aina sat with her mother till she had fallen asleep, then she also lay down with her mother and slept. Before sleeping her last coherent thought was, "I may never see my brother Laila again."

But she was wrong. Laila came running inside the house just a week afterwards. They were all in the courtyard. They froze as they saw Laila who was crying loudly. Everyone ran out to find out what the problem was. Daadi shouted, "Why are you coming here? Why are you crying?"

Rukmini was the most worried. She said, "What is the matter? Why are you crying? Speak quickly."

Laila screamed, "Oh! Munni bai is dead. Your Sudha is dead."

Parwati asked, "How do you know that she was our Sudha?"

Laila answered, "She told me herself. I feel so sad for her. She must have been murdered."

"What! How! Oh!" and Rukmini began to cry.

Even Prasad looked upset, but he ordered his wife, "Stop crying. Let us hear what has happened."

Laila said, "It was a bad night yesterday. The Nawab was made to drink a lot of wine. In that intoxicated condition he was made to sign some property papers. In the night he died. Sudha came to know about his death. She was in her house when a man came and showed her the will of the late Nawab. Even her palace had been gifted to the Nawab's youngest wife. Sudha refused to leave the property that was in her name. She said that she would fight it in court."

"Then what happened? Speak quickly," said Prasad.

"Then in the morning she was found burnt. Nobody knows what happened. The police is saying that she committed suicide but the servants in her palace say that it was murder, because she was found sitting against the kitchen door. How can a person who is burning, sit quietly? The pain of the burning should have made her move around. It seems that the youngest wife of the Nawab is responsible because all the property of the Nawab is now hers. I must go now."

"I want to go and see my daughter," sobbed Rukmini, as Laila walked away.

"No, you will not go there," said Prasad.

"What a father you are! There may be no one there to claim her body," cried Rukmini.

Prasad looked uncertain. He asked Mahavir, "Do you think I should go to claim Sudha's body?"

Daadi spoke up, "While she was living Sudha did not want to reveal that she was the daughter of this house. Why do you want it known after her death?"

They all looked at Mahavir. The final decision was his. Aina too looked at her Baba hoping that he would live up to the expectations she had from him. She willed him to say that Sudha would be given a decent funeral by her own family. But it was not to be. Mahavir just walked away. He would not listen to anyone, not even Aina, who felt let down as never before.

She felt as if Baba was not the demi-god that she had made him out to be. He was just an ordinary mortal who did not have the courage even to stand up for his womenfolk. And because of the stubborn refusal of Daadi and Baba, and the taken-for-granted obedience of Prasad to what his elder brother said, no one budged from the house that day. Rukmini had pleaded and begged in vain. She had run out of the house saying that she would go to her daughter, but she had fallen down and had hurt her head. She had lain unconscious the whole day. So no one went to claim the body of Sudha.

Thus the body of Sudha was taken away by the municipal authorities and cremated finally, after no one came to claim the dead body. When Rukmini was better the next day, she cried a lot. Finally Veena came and she said to Rukmini, "It is good that Sudha is dead. She was suffering so much. Atleast she will be happy with God in Heaven. Atleast He will be a true Father and not forsake His own child."

"This is all kismat," said Prasad.

"This is murder of an innocent and you all are responsible for it. My poor child had to suffer throughout her life because of you all," said Rukmini.

Mahavir said, "I know that this is tragic but, it would be best, if this is not spoken about again.'

Aina said, "Baba. This is not something one can forget."

Mahavir looked stunned. He said, "What do you mean Aina?"

Aina shouted, "Sudha Bua was a daughter of the house. How despicable that her life and her end were so tragic and lonely. You have failed, all of you. You could not take care of the daughter that God sent you; rather you defiled a daughter by your narrow thinking. You tell me not to cry, but you force us girls to cry throughout a lifetime. I hate you all, most of all you Baba. If you could feel for women, why couldn't you make sure that not a single girl in your own family was troubled by life? Why didn't you teach them to hit out and give it back to those who hurt them? But I will. If anyone troubles me, I will not tolerate it like Sudha Bua. I will retaliate on my own."

"Rant all you want here, girl, but don't talk about it again," said Daadi.

Aina's mother Gomti pulled Aina by the hair and took her inside her room.

Gomti shouted, "You have really grown a rude tongue. You have forgotten your promise to me. I order you from today that you will obey what is told to you. You have to listen to others and stop this rebellious spirit of yours. You have to swear on me again that you will never be rebellious but you will always keep up the family prestige. If you don't, you will see my dead face."

"If the elders do something wrong, can't we bring it to their notice?" questioned Aina.

"No you cannot. You have to respect them. They will do what is right according to the norms of society." "What society are you talking of? We make the society. If you change, then the others will change too," said Aina.

"Just shut up. Now touch me and swear that you will never go against the accepted norms of the family and the society. Swear that you will never rebel or I will be dead," said her Ma and she forced Aina to keep her hand on her head. Aina finally gave the promise to her mother and forced herself to try and forget poor Sudha, because Sudha's memory always made her heart ache.

So Sudha was seemingly forgotten by all except in her mother's heart. But then Girish, Sabal and Prabal came as soon as they were given the news of their sister Sudha's death by Prasad, by a trunk call from the local Telegraph office. Girish was mad with fury at the turn of events and this time he was in no mood to keep quiet.

He started raging at Mahavir, "I came to know about Sudha just some years back. You are the one who took this decision about Sudha. Why? You never understand the pain you give us. You have always done what you wanted with us. You dictate and my father listens to you. It has always upset me that my father, mother and we children I, Prabal and Sabal, are nothing but puppets in your hands. I really hate this situation. I feel trapped. What would you do if Aina is made a prostitute? Would you turn her out of the house? You had done a great injustice to Sudha by turning her out of the house. Now was the time to make up. But you played God again. Atleast you could have given her a proper funeral and honestly announced to the world that she was a daughter of this house. Why didn't you?"

"Sudha wanted to hide this fact herself," said Daadi.

Girish was furious. In a rage he shouted, "That was because Sudha was such a good individual, but what about your duty, Parwati Devi? I hate you and I hate you too Mahavir Chandra. I feel like hurting you both as much as you have hurt us. Mahavir Chandra. You are very fond of your granddaughter Aina. What if I kill her and then leave her forsaken and lonely body for the Municipal Corporation to take and cremate?"

"Shut up," shouted Prasad.

Girish shouted, "Papa. I won't shut up now. I am fed up of this life of being bonded like a slave to your elder brother. He did not let me marry the girl I loved more than my life. I wish he suffers a lot."

And Mahavir swayed as he stood. Before he could speak anything more, suddenly Mahavir caught his chest, slumped and fell. The doctor was called, and he diagnosed it as a heart attack.

The house seemed to come to a standtill till Mahavir was out of the critical list. No one spoke of Sudha. It did finally seem that Sudha's chapter would be closed. But the mother Rukmini did not let anyone forget what they had done to Sudha. Prasad came in front of his elder brother after a couple of days. He was visibly upset and for the first time he seemed to be in a state of confused indecision. Then stammering, he told his brother, "We want to leave this house, forever."

Mahavir shouted, "Are you out of your mind? How can you think of going out from your own house? Things have happened, but we can sort them out."

Prasad said, "I can't help it. Oh! Please forgive me, but we have to go. It hurts me and I know that it will hurt you also, but please let us go."

"Where will you go?" asked Mahavir.

"We will stay with Girish, Sabal and Prabal in the city. I can't help it. Rukmini and Girish will not listen to reason any more. They both are very upset about Sudha. Please forgive me, but could I get my portion of the property, because I have no source of income."

Mahavir in his heart, knew that he was guilty and so he did not stop Prasad and his wife. He called his lawyer. He discussed with them their portion of the property and the papers were signed. Prasad put that part of the house on rent. Gomti and Kalka had to vacate their room and shift into the room occupied by Prasad and his wife. And Aina's Prasad baba and Rukmini Amma with Girish, Sabal and Prabal finally went away to live in Lucknow. It was a parting where Aina saw her Baba actually breakdown and cry like an inconsolable baby for the first time in her life. Mahavir had never cried like this ever in his life, but now he cried for his brother.

Prasad touched his feet and gruffly Mahavir embraced him, but Rukmini was unrepentant. She had her head covered. She just walked away without meeting anyone. Girish, Sabal and Prabal also kept quiet and walked off with their parents. It was a final break. No one knew if they would ever meet again.

CHAPTER 20

The whole house became curiously silent after their departure, though there were still many people in it. The most hit was Mahavir. Both the brothers Mahavir and Prasad had always had a deep understanding and love. Mahavir had felt responsible for Prasad's family also. Now he lost his zest for life. He hated to see his family break up. He suddenly looked old and weary.

He couldn't even face Aina because she always looked accusingly at him. Even after time passed and was supposed to heal, Aina could not forgive anyone for the way they had behaved with Sudha.

Then their extended family ganged up against the sick Mahavir with the demand that everyone should be given their portion of the property just as Prasad had been given. Mahavir shrank before this onslaught.

One day he called his lawyer and had the whole property divided. Everyone was willing to take their share, but no one was ready to shoulder the debts. All the families wanted separate rooms and kitchens. Soon many households replaced the one big joint family and it smote Mahavir's heart. And then the exodus started.

Many cousins sold their portion and moved to the city where opportunities and more money tempted the people. Many strangers now lived in the areas where once his near and dear ones had lived. Now only Aina, her Ma and her Papa were left in their part of the house, with a separate kitchen. Baba and Daadi stayed with them, but they were now unhappy and depressed.

On Prasad's insistence, Munna still stayed with him in the city. That was a balm to the emotionally wounded Mahavir. His brother was still full of love for him. Inspite of whatever had happened, he was still ready to look after Munna.

The break up of the family was too much for Daadi to take and she became too weak to get up and then one day the defeated Mahavir put his trembling hand on her forehead and said to his wife, "Parwati. Please become well again. I cannot live without you. Please don't die before me. I won't be able to live alone. Let me die before you."

It seemed as if this gave Parwati the will to live. She started taking her medicines and forced herself to eat well. She started feeling better.

One day another incident rocked the already weakened household. The eunuch Basanti came to the house from the back entrance as she used to. She knocked at the back door thinking that Gomti would respond, but there were tenants living in it.

That room had been given away to Prasad and he had given his portion to a family on rent. The tenant's family started shouting, 'Help! Help! Thieves!' the moment they heard Basanti tapping on the window. The family caught Basanti and brought her to Baba.

The tenant said, "You are a weird family. An eunuch comes in the middle of the night and knocks at our door to meet a woman of your family."

Basanti saw Mahavir and said, "I have come to meet your daughter-in-law Gomti. Call your daughter-in-law and ask her. I used to come and meet her."

Mahavir was totally shocked but first he asked the tenants to go. Then Aina saw her mother walking upto Baba. She was trembling. Aina hated seeing her like this. Basanti screamed, "Please tell them that I am not a thief and that I used to come to meet you."

"Why would an eunuch come to meet my daughter-in-law in the middle of the night? Basanti I will send you to jail," said Mahavir.

Basanti said, "No please don't. You can't do this to me. The fact is that your daughter-in-law gave birth to a son who was an eunuch. Laila is the son of Gomti. I kept him and looked after him."

Before anyone could do anything, Mahavir fell down dead of a massive heart attack.

Basanti got scared and ran away. Kalka stood stupefied looking at the dead body of his father lying on the floor. All he could do was mumble, "Oh! What have we done!" Everyone was so stunned by the turn of events that no one afterwards thought of questioning Gomti about what had happened and when, and why she had not told anyone about Laila.

Daadi was past crying. She only said, "He wanted to go before me and see I have kept my promise. I am alive to see this wretched world, but he has got an escape from this hell."

Kalka was for the first time the head of the family. He felt lost. Till now he had left everything to his father, but now he realized that he would have to take decisions. This was entirely new to him and filled him with a lot of fear, but then he started thinking of his problems coherently. Before anything, money had to be collected for the cremation of his father. No one helped him. Thoroughly disappointed, his feet led him to Bijli.

He had thought that he would just spend some hours of quiet with her, but Bijli saw that he was very perturbed. When she came to know the facts, she went in and got a small bag filled with money.

Bijli said, "Take this money. This is all I have."

Kalka said, "How can I take this money? This is all that you have for your old age."

"You have given me enough Kalka. True love means giving and I really love you."

Tears poured down Kalka's cheeks as he said, "Bijli, I have always taken from you."

Bijli said, "Hush! Please go and look after your family and remind Aina of the chant I had told her."

Kalka could only nod. He held her tightly. Bijli clung to him but then she moved out of his embrace and pushed him towards the door.

Prasad came for the cremation of his brother Mahavir, but Rukmini refused to come. She could not forgive Daadi and Baba. Aina became like a statue. She felt a shock and she would not believe that her Baba was dead. But somehow his death did not touch her.

For her, the day he had forsaken Sudha's dead body, he had fallen from a very high pedestal and his statue had been completely broken in her mind. She would imagine the dead body of Sudha lying alone and being carried in a Municipal truck, and she would cringe. She would get nightmares of Sudha's dead body crying out, "Don't forsake me. Don't leave me please." She would get up sweating profusely. She too found it very difficult to pardon her Baba and Daadi.

Daadi seemed to have lost her will to live too. She would just sit on a cot on one side of the open courtyard. Then peacefully Daadi died in her sleep after a month.

Aina was shattered but then she thought that in a way, death had been a deliverance for both her Daadi and Baba. This made her accept their deaths with more fortitude. Yet she felt a vacuum in her life. When all the guests had gone, then Rukmini came, because now both Baba and Daadi were not there, and her grouse had been against them. She had become very thin and listless. She cried after embracing Aina and her mother. She stayed for a few hours and then returned to the city.

A year of mourning started. There could be no marriage or any auspicious celebration for the whole year till a ritual was done after the eleventh month to finish the mourning. Now Kalka, Gomti and Aina were left and Munna would come off and on. Aina suddenly had matured as the cruel slaps of fate had shaken her world. Kalka looked for a job but he could not get it. The money that Bijli had given Kalka, had got finished in the urgent debts and the cremations of Baba and Daadi.

The lack of money could not be sidetracked any more. They were poor. Aina left her studies because money had to be sent to Munna. Then came their saviour. A man came and gave them a thousand rupees, saying that this was for Aina and was to be used for the house. The man did not tell them who had sent the money. Gomti felt that it must be the Rai family who had sent repeated proposals for Aina. From then, every month, they would get one thousand rupees.

The barber's wife again brought a proposal from the Rai family. Gomti asked the barber's wife, "Why do the Rais want Daman to marry Aina?"

"The fact is that they are from an ordinary family. They want the son to marry an educated girl from an aristocratic background like yours. They think she will adjust better because she is from a joint family."

"How many people stay in that house?" asked Gomti.

"Daman and his mother Ram Katori and another person Heera who looks after their business but he is not family.No one will trouble her as just the mother-in-law and her husband will be with Aina."

Aina was against her marriage because she was worried that her mother would have no one to care for her. Then one day, her mother became seriously ill. She told Aina, "This house seems to have a curse on it. Now your father has started drinking a lot again. I want you to promise that when you get married, call Munna to your place and keep him and his family with you if I die."

Gomti burst out crying, her weak body wracked by heart rending sobs. Aina felt it very unfair on her mother's part to consider only the welfare of Munna, but Gomti left no option for her and Aina had to agree. Gomti had another wish that Aina should be married because Gomti may die, which Aina could not refuse.

Aina's father Kalka was sent to the Rai household by Gomti, who had taken a promise from him that he would definitely fix Aina's wedding with Daman Rai. And Kalka did just that. The marriage was settled. The family was happy that the boy and his mother did not want any dowry and the wedding was just the next week. Gomti was beside herself with joy, so she asked Kalka, "Why are you so serious? Is anything wrong?"

Kalka said, "I did not feel happy there, though they are rich. The 'boy' is tall and slim but he looks funny somehow and he seems to be too old for Aina. The mother-in-law seems very sharp and clever. I didn't feel comfortable with them. I don't think they will keep Aina well. I am afraid for her. I felt as if the boy didn't want to get married. Don't get Aina married there."

Gomti replied, "Don't say another word. This marriage has to take place. They will keep her well, don't worry. Money is our problem and if we don't marry Aina just now, she might not get married at all and what would a girl do without marriage? If she doesn't get married, she will be a burden on Munna and Sonali always. So we have to get her married now. Just keep quiet."

When Aina came to know that her marriage was fixed, she felt frustrated and trapped. She was caught between her first instinct of rebelling and the expected conservative tradition of obedience that had been so ingrained in her by the elders. She could not move out of the net of custom and the need to cater to the elders.

CHAPTER 21

Aina may have felt very afraid of getting married to Daman Rai, but everyone behaved as if Aina had no say in the matter. Aina felt as if she was just a utensil to be sent to another house. No one asked her.

Gomti called Veena and said, "You are the eldest now, so please tell us what we should do."

Veena said, "I would say that together you get Aina married and also do the 'Gauna' ceremony of Munna to bring his wife here. In this way the cost will be less and after Aina goes, Sonali can look after you."

Aina said to Veena Amma, "I will marry on one condition that you will fully participate in my wedding. You cannot be inauspicious for me. Rather I think that you are lucky for me."

Veena felt really happy and she agreed. She then, for the first time, helped Gomti with the wedding preparations. Rukmini was also informed and she came. All the three women were anxious as to where the money would come from. The next morning, a boy came and gave Aina twenty thousand rupees to spend for her wedding. The women were delighted and they were sure that Daman Rai had sent the money. Now everything was done in a hurry.

The Rais wanted a short wedding. So it was fixed that there would be just one dinner Reception and in the night Aina would be sent to her in-law's place.

It was also decided that Munna would go and get his wife Sonali home. The relatives went to Sonali's house with Munna and Sonali was brought to their house in Najapur and just as she walked in with Munna, the eunuchs came. Basanti was not with them.

Aina saw Laila with them and understood that Laila must have joined the eunuchs' group. The eunuchs started singing and dancing. Gomti was very perturbed and she told her husband Kalka to quickly give money to the eunuchs and tell them to go. Then she went ahead to welcome Sonali in the traditional way. Sonali was basically a city girl who did not care for old customs.

When Sonali came, it was a shock to everyone. She did not cover her head at all. She brought a small pomenarian dog with her that shocked the cleanliness minded women of the household. She did not care for anyone's feelings. Sonali said with disgust, "What is all this fuss about my coming here? I am tired and I want to rest. Where is my bedroom?"

There was a shocked silence but Sonali took the hand of Munna and Munna took her towards the room meant to be their bedroom. Gomti kept waiting, standing to welcome Sonali in the traditional way.

From that day Sonali created havoc with the sentiments of the old fashioned people. She said she didn't like anything there. She never obeyed anyone. She wouldn't cook or work in the house. She told them to keep servants for the household chores.

She also answered back, even to elders and that was a sacrilege and a blasphemy in their household, because youngsters as a sacred rule had to obey the elders, come what may. And Munna could do nothing. He was totally henpecked.

Gomti was dismayed when she saw the behaviour of Sonali because Sonali did not look after her. Everyone had thought that Sonali would take over the cooking and look after her sick mother-in-law, but Sonali did no housework. Rather Sonali expected everyone to look after her.

Sonali was full of tantrums too. Once Aina felt the sharp edge of her tongue. Aina for the first time was happy that she was getting married and going away.

The day of Aina's wedding came. Many relatives did not attend, though they were still living in the same palace. The rest of the relatives present there tried to sing and dance, trying to re-capture the merriment they were used to, but their past happiness was just elusive. Everyone began crying, thinking about their old glory when the whole family was together.

The 'baraat' came and the guests were made to sit in the open courtyard in their portion of the palace. The bridegroom had not been seen by anyone of the family except Kalka. The disenchanted bridegroom looked quite old, surly and irritated, and the women of the house started, pitying poor Aina.

Ram Katori dictated whatever ceremonies had to take place and Gomti and Kalka merely tried to appease her. When the wedding party sat down for dinner, they irritated Aina's family very much. Munna came and told Rukmini Amma that the guests were really troubling everyone and making fun of everyone. He said that one young man Manav was leading the rest of the people in creating problems. He was very handsome but he seemed to order even Daman around.

Munna came to the kitchen and said to his mother, "Ma. I will teach them a lesson."

His mother said, "No, they are from the boy's party and they might get angry."

But Rukmini gave him red chilli powder which Munna mixed with whatever they served to the troublemakers. Then it was real fun watching all the troublemakers looking for water and sweets to quell the burning of their mouths, but the friend Manav started shouting, "These rogues have dared to give us red chilli and Daman you are not doing anything about this? You should teach them a lesson."

The bridegroom Daman became angry and he started walking away saying, "I will not marry." Aina's father Kalka and brother Munna had to apologize, then only did Daman sit down again to get married.

Aina went out to join her bridegroom Daman when she was called for the wedding rituals. When the priest asked her parents to give her hand in Daman's hand, Aina didn't like the touch of his hand at all.

Then it was time for Aina to go away from her house. Aina cried her heart out because she had caught one glimpse of her husband and not liked him at all.

He was tall and slim but his face had narrow harsh eyes, a long hooked nose and thin lips. He was not handsome; rather, he seemed effeminate and on top of that he had a contemptuous and snobbish look as if all of the people there were below his status.

Gomti also cried a lot but not because of Aina's departure. She had the fear that her future would be very unpredictable because of the temperament of Sonali. Before leaving, Aina met every family member and they burst out crying at her plight.

Aina pleaded, "Please don't send me. I am afraid."

Aina started trembling and she clung to Gomti and said, "I won't go. Ma keep me with you. Don't send me." But ofcourse Aina had to go, but the family could not forget her tear-ravaged face as she was made to follow Daman and was taken to a decorated car.

It was cool and beautiful. Just like Aina, the dawn seemed to tiptoe like a blushing bride on the periphery of the sky. Suddenly someone screamed. Everyone rushed towards the bus in which the marriage party was going, where a lady had screamed. Aina's parents, Daman and his mother and her other relatives left her there and went to see what had happened.

Aina felt utterly and devastatingly alone. She realized that now her family members would not be there to protect her. There was so much turmoil inside her, that Aina started feeling panic. She started trembling and she felt herself sinking down into a deep abyss.

Then she became conscious of a male body holding her upright and suddenly she felt very secure. She rested her head on his shoulder. A soft male voice said, "Are you all right, Lady? Now don't faint again. Take deep breaths and you will not feel the tension so much. Everything will be all right, so don't worry."

The voice and the touch were like a balm and Aina quietened down. She took deep breaths and that certainly helped her. She tried to see to whom the soothing voice belonged, but her long veil made it impossible for her to see. He disentangled himself and Aina felt bereft. She kept straining her ears to hear that voice again, but in vain. Moreover she had loved his touch. She wanted to feel it again. It did not repulse her at all. It was a touch that made her tingle, yet feel nice.

It was comforting, yet exciting. "Why did the man have to set me free so soon?" she thought despondently.

She suddenly felt a strong yearning for his firm but gentle touch again. But by then it had been found out that an aunt had slipped and hurt herself. After tending to her, the marriage party sat in the bus finally, and the bus moved. Daman, his mother Ram Katori and a friend came to sit in the car with Aina. That voice did not belong to her husband or his friend.

She could not see them because of her long and thick veil. But she heard them because after sitting in the car, Daman said to his mother in an extremely irritated voice, "What a farce you have got me into, Mataji (Mother), just to keep up an appearance before society. Now I am saddled with a wife for a lifetime."

Ram Katori, her mother-in-law answered, "Hush! I told you to be careful. Don't talk."

The friend said, "Now it is over, my dear friend. Now you are in control of your destiny."

Ram Katori hissed, "Both of you shut up. Not a word more."

They fell silent. After that nothing was spoken in the car which was driven for about two hours. Aina was so tired that she fell asleep. Even in her sleepy state, she realised that whenever she swerved even just a little towards Daman, he would push her away roughly.

They reached their destination. She was rudely awakened by Ram Katori and told to step outside the car. Aina had reached her in-law's home and Aina was really impressed by the palatial house. She was welcomed inside by some female relatives.

"My new house is certainly grand. Swami Ram was correct in saying that I would have money, but he had also said that there would be catastrophes. God save me," thought Aina.

There was the opulent fragrance of wealth everywhere, extra pleasant to Aina after the difficult times she had suffered in the last few years. It also made her forget the detached and unemotional behaviour of her husband in the car. She decided to forget her premonition. She thought that now her life would be happy and without problems.

She thought too soon.

Aina was told to change her clothes and get ready at once. She was taken downstairs. Aina was famished and thirsty, but no one bothered to even ask her whether she wanted anything to eat or drink, and she could not ask them. Moreover it was also humiliating to hear comments like "her features are good but your daughter-in-law is dark. Your son deserved a better wife." Other women remarked, "She is not so good looking. I hope she has brought a good dowry to compensate her lack of looks and beauty."

Ram Katori would answer, "Oh no! She has brought nothing."

Another woman commented, "She looks quite old. Girls should be married young."

Ram Katori said defensively, "She is in her early twenties only, which is good as the law now allows girls to be married only after eighteen years."

The woman replied, "Well Daman is quite old." Ram Katori was lost for words as it was a fact, but her sister replied, "A man's age does not matter. It is better when the man is mature."

After that the whole day Aina kept sitting as someone or the other would come to see her. Then she was shifted to another room where the bridal bed was decorated. The ladies of the house came laughing and giggling all the time and inspected the bridal bed which was decorated with beautiful flowers.

There were a lot of teasing comments that made Aina blush in embarrassment and she felt thankful for the long veil on her face. She was then made to sit on the bridal bed, to wait for her husband.

The fragrance of the flowers made her feel pleasant and her mind reminded her of the voice and touch of the person who had supported her near the flower-decked car. What happiness she would have felt if he had been her husband. She started imagining what it would be like when he came, but she was so tired, that after waiting for some time, she fell asleep.

And she started seeing a nightmare. She saw a man coming in into her room. She was about to scream when he put a hand on her mouth and told her to shut up. She hated his touch, but she had heard the voice somewhere. Then suddenly she felt that someone was tugging at her clothes in the dark. She felt livid. She shouted to her mother for help but her mother didn't come to help. Then she struggled to free herself from the monster whose touch was so rough and hurtful.

She froze. She felt fear in every cell of her body. She felt that she must stop him. Now she would not take it any more. She was an adult and she could fend for herself. She felt the monster's cruel hands holding her wrist. His roughness grated on her nerves. She felt a rage sweeping her. These men. They were worse than brutes. She would show them.

Her Baba had told her to resist and chuck away anyone who forced himself on her. So she decided that she would not take this torture any more. With all her strength Aina yanked herself onto one side and pushed the monster off the bed. She did not know from where she got the strength, but she refused to be submissive.

The man rolled onto the floor with a scream and a thud and she was free. She had been balanced precariously between the nightmare and reality, but the thud made her regain full consciousness.

Then her mind cleared enough for her to remember that she was married and this man may well have been her husband demanding his conjugal rights. It might have been her husband falling onto the floor and then walking away, because she had seen a figure going out of the door. She sat up. She felt really frightened.

Oh what had she done? She should have dutifully done what her mother had instructed her, to obey and make it easier for her husband. With sheer nerves she felt like screaming, because she was afraid that her husband might get angry for throwing him off like this. But he did not come back.

"Why did he have to come in the dark? Is he afraid to show me his face? Maybe he was embarassed and that is why he did not put on the light. Did I imagine it? No. I am sure it was happening. It is not a dream."

Suddenly she was thankful that he had gone away from the room. Out of fear she could not sleep after that, but spent the night anticipating dangers even in the shadows. The loneliness hurt her, as before her marriage she had lived in a joint family, where there were so many people all the time.

CHAPTER 22

When she got up in the morning, she quickly got ready. Soon a servant came and told her that her mother-in-law was calling her downstairs.

Aina went down, only to hear Ram Katori's nasty taunt, "So are you a queen that you will take so long to come down? Now start cooking breakfast."

Aina obeyed her and after that she found herself obeying her mother-in-law throughout the day, without anyone giving her anything to eat and drink. First it was breakfast, then lunch, right upto dinner for which Daman came very late. It was past midnight when Aina reached her room. Again her husband did not come to her room in the night. The next few days again added to her woes as she realized that her in-law's house would be like a prison for her and she was supposed to be like a dumb puppet, who had come to do housework. Her mother-in-law made Aina slog. Aina started feeling tired.

After doing such a lot of work, her mother-in-law kept taunting her. "Oh God! I have to bear with such a girl who has not been taught anything. You are a useless pest. Why did I have to get my eligible son married to you? I am unlucky that you are my daughter-in-law."

Aina was nervous on one count. She was afraid to meet her husband after the first night. He came the next evening to their room, but acted as if the first night had not happened at all. He just shifted the two single beds farther away and the only words that he spoke to her were, "That is your bed and this is mine. Please don't touch my bed at all." So that was the punishment.

He would not make love to her or touch her at all. Aina didn't know what to feel. For some reason her mind told her that she was quite relieved that he would not force himself on her again. She still covered her head with her veil, but now she could see him and she did not like what she saw. His looks were not even average, as he was a replica of his mother and there was a ruthlessness and stubbornness in the set of his jaws and sneering lips, which seemed to threaten her, because he looked at her with something akin to hatred.

Aina even kept quiet when Ram Katori tried to keep her away from Daman. Ram Katori interfered a lot in her relationship with her husband. It almost seemed as if her mother-in-law was making sure that Aina would have no privacy with her husband. At times she would come in the morning and go late at night from their room when Daman was at home. Sometimes she would show as if she was very tired and she would fall asleep on their bed. Aina was very irritated with the ploys that Ram Katori used to try to keep Aina away from Daman, but after a time she was glad of this interference, because even when Daman was in their room, he would negate her very presence and insult her whenever he could.

One day Daman's aunt Suryakumari came visiting and asked Ram Katori, "Did you take your daughter-in-law to the temple?"

When Ram Katori answered in the negative, Suryakumari insisted that Aina should go to the temple with Daman. And they went in the family carriage.

Aina thought, "I had thought that I would own a carriage, but at what cost have I got it."

That night Suryakumari walked into their room. "What!" she screamed. "Why are your beds put away from each other? Daman? This is not done. I want your child in this house within nine months."

She called a servant and joined the two single beds. She then said to Daman, "In the night I will come to verify. Remember that."

Daman knew that his aunt was capable of peeping through the keyhole, so he did not shift the beds again. That night he talked to Aina. In the past most of the time he would go to sleep the moment his head touched a pillow, but that day he lay down and asked brusquely, "Why did you push me off the bed?"

Aina remained quiet and Daman continued, "I had no desire to come to you, but my relatives forced me to. I hated touching you, but when against my will, I came towards you, you had the temerity to chuck me off the bed. Don't you have any decency that you treat your husband like that on the first night? As a punishment I will not touch you till you say sorry to me."

He waited for Aina to apologise. Aina thought, "If this is my punishment, why am I feeling so relieved? I really don't want him to touch me, so I will not apologise to him till I can bring myself to like his touch. Thank you very much, my husband, for giving me a reprieve. I don't like you anyway." When Aina did not apologise, Daman turned his back towards her and went to sleep.

Next morning, the grind of the housework and the taunts began again. And so it went on. Aina hated it. She despised being on the receiving end. She had always thought that she would never let herself get exploited, but now she was torn between her desire not to get exploited and her promise to her mother that she would compromise. She suffered in silence. It was hard to live this kind of existence. But one voice . . . . the gentle, soothing voice . . . kept her going.

Through the long veil, she had not been able to see all the men and women of the family. They were relatives who, afterwards went away from Ram Katori's house. Except that one male voice. The same very soft, tender and loving voice. The voice that answered to the name of Heera. 'Heera' meaning diamond.

She had heard the voice off and on, but she had not been able to see to whom it belonged. But it was a voice she waited for. She yearned to have its smooth enveloping warmth comfort her. That voice was her one anchor. She held on to it to keep her sanity.

She often thought, "Is it possible to fall in love with a voice?" She knew the answer. Yes. She herself had fallen in love with the voice, but it was wrong, as she was already married. And then came the day Aina met the man behind the voice. Aina had been working since morning without being given anything to eat or drink. She stood still as she suddenly heard that voice say to Ram Katori, "Madam, why do you trouble your new daughter-in-law so much?"

"What has that got to do with you? You are an accountant, so just remain that. Don't try to show familiarity with the family. She is my daughter-in-law. I will do as I want," said Ram Katori.

Heera said, "She has come from another house and you have put her to work and how much work? From morning till night she is just slogging. She is a human being. This is not fair."

"Shut up Heera. Mind your own business," said Ram Katori.

"My father had served your family so well before he died, that your husband thought of him as his younger brother. It is my business to see that you treat your daughter-in-law well," said Heera, but Ram Katori brushed him off rudely by saying, "Shut up."

After some days, Aina was alone in the house. Ram Katori had gone to a neighbour's house to mourn someone's death. The same kind voice called her, "Listen lady? May I have a word with you?"

Aina walked to the door of her room with the veil on her face. Heera came in and said, "Lady. Has Madam given the keys of the safe to you? I need money from the safe to pay some bills urgently."

Aina just shook her head because it was firmly embedded in her bones that she should not speak to any man other than those closely related to her.

Heera laughed, "Ofcourse Madam would not give you the keys. She is a miser. She doesn't trust anyone. I manage the funds so she has to trust me. I am unhappy that she treats you so badly. I can realize also that Daman does not care for you. You must be feeling so lonely but you just go on working without complaining. I respect that. If you need anything, ask me."

After such a long time she had heard caring words, said in a tender voice, so Aina burst out crying. She tried to check her tears but she couldn't. Then she felt a hand on her shoulder. His touch. Firm yet gentle, dependable and reliable. And kind. It matched the voice of Heera and was greatly comforting, just as she had remembered it from the first time she had felt it.

Then she heard his voice say gently, "Cry all you want, lady. I know how tough it must be for you. I can understand how much you are suffering."

He put his arm around Aina and she kept her head on his shoulder and cried. Without realising it, she moved closer to him. Suddenly she felt that she was no longer hurting inside. Rather she was feeling quite nice. Why? Because she was in Heera's arms and she liked the feeling. Actually she loved the feeling. Without her being conscious of it, her hand had reached his back, the muscles firm but smooth through his thin shirt.

Aina realized that for the first time, she felt at home. She felt as if she had reached the destination that she had been searching for. She felt one of his arms holding her tightly and the other caressing her hair. Her sobs subsided as she became aware of being pressed against his body which was warm and comforting. She felt as if she could hold him close to her for a lifetime.

She realized that she wanted more. She felt that she was doing something that the world would consider a sin, but for her it seemed very natural. She suddenly looked up and her veil fell back. He saw her for the first time and he gasped. He was stunned by her beauty. He stared at her for a long time memorising the outline of her features. The shapely nose set between attractive, drugged eyes, still wet with tears. Her bow lips parted with surprise as she too saw him clearly for the first time.

Heera gasped, "Daman is a fool. He does not realize what a precious diamond he has got. You are just lovely, lady, but very young. Too young for Daman. Oh Lord! How could your parents marry you to a person like Daman? But Lady, you are really beautiful."

"How do you call me beautiful? My Ma says that I am dark," said Aina.

Heera said, "That is just the right complexion to go with your sharp features. You are enchanting, though I shouldn't be saying this."

Aina said, "Thank you." And she was thinking, "He is so fair and handsome. I like his shapely but strong features also. I like his big eyes and long eyelashes and the wave of his hair falling across his forehead. The best is that there is decency in his eyes. He appears reliable, responsible and ever so adorable."

"Lady, I want to ask you one thing. Why do you let yourself suffer at the hands of your mother-in-law?"

"There is nothing wrong in doing work in the house. All women do housework," answered Aina.

"Not in this house. Lady, your mother-in-law never ever lifted a utensil even. She never worked. There were servants to do all the housework. She chucked out three servants before you came."

"Thank you for telling me," replied Aina. "Where do you stay?" she asked.

"I live in this house only. I have been given the last room down the next corridor," replied Heera.

He led her to the chair and made her sit down. As she realized how much she had liked his touch on her body, she also realized how much she had hated Daman's touch on her body. Heera left her to get a glass of water for her and Aina suddenly felt deprived. But he came back and they talked for a long time. It seemed the most natural thing for her to be with Heera. It was as if she belonged to him and he belonged to her.

Aina suddenly asked, "How are you like this?"

"What do you mean, lady?" asked Heera.

"You are so kind. Till now I thought that all men were unkind. Well except my Baba, but then he also showed himself unkind to my Sudha bua. You are so different. You seem warm and caring," said Aina.

"You must have met the wrong type of men till now," said Heera, with a smile.

Aina asked, "Why do you call my mother-in-law Madam? That means that she is your boss."

Heera said, "She is my boss because she gives me a salary, but I am not a servant. I belong to a very good family. My father was very close to her husband. Her husband had shown many obligations to my father, so I thought that I should repay them. Otherwise I am educated and can get a job elsewhere."

Just then they heard the voice of Ram Katori coming into the house and Heera walked out of her room. She heard Ram Katori say to Heera, "What are you doing here?"

"I needed money so I came to ask your daughter-in-law for the keys, but ofcourse you would never give your keys to her. She is your arch enemy."

"Stop it, and listen to me smart guy. You are young and a bachelor. Don't ever come near the room of my daughter-in-law or I will sack you," said Ram Katori.

"What else can you do! You need puppets who dance to your tune always. You have sacked everyone except a few servants. That is why you have been left alone. There will be a time when you will be left fully and completely alone. Don't treat me like a servant because I am ready to go away anytime. I will go away happily. Should I give my resignation just now?" asked Heera.

"Oh! You can't even take a joke, Heera," said Ram Katori sheepishly.

"Madam, you need me and because my father had wanted me to work here, so I am here. I can get a very good job if I go away from here," said Heera.

"Ofcourse Heera," said Ram Katori meekly.

Next morning, Aina got up late and took her time getting ready. A maid servant banged at her door repeatedly on the instructions of Ram Katori but Aina did not answer. After an hour, Aina walked downstairs to see that Ram Katori was raging mad.

As soon as Aina came down, she asked, "Why are you so late today?"

"I got up late, Sasuma.(mother-in-law)"

"Why?" hissed Ram Katori, surprised that Aina had answered back.

"That is simple. Because I slept late. Girdhari, come here. Cook breakfast for me."

Ram Katori shouted, "But Girdhari is Daman's personal valet. You get up and do your work."

"Why don't you get more servants? Sasuma, is it because you have no money?"

"Shut up. How dare you. Ofcourse we have money," shouted Ram Katori.

"Then get more servants," answered Aina politely.

Aina was not prepared for the scene that followed. Ram Katori started howling and crying loudly.

Daman came running and Ram Katori shrieked, "This wife of yours has insulted me. She has been so rude and impudent. Daman, aren't you man enough to keep one woman in check?"

Naturally this instigated Daman to prove his masculinity. He grabbed Aina's hands and dragged her into their room. He threw her on to the bed and shouted, "You will stay here till you learn how to speak politely to my mother. Nothing will be given to you to eat or drink. You better learn good manners and politeness."

Aina replied, "I will not obey you. I will do as I please. Keep more servants for the housework. Till now I listened to you and your mother but now I refuse to be a bonded slave whatever you may say or do with me."

"You will do as my mother and I say."

"No, I will not. Enough is enough and tell your mother not to bad mouth and taunt me. She should learn to be polite. I will not take rubbish from both of you."

Daman strode towards her and caught her hands, growling, "You have to be obedient and totally subservient to us. I will throttle you if you disobey us."

Aina retorted, "What else can you do? Men are nothing but brutes and when they see no way out, they just show brute force. But I refuse to be exploited here."

CHAPTER 23

Daman was now in a very bad mood. He was very angry and shouted at her, "Yes you are right. I will show you brute force. Here take it. You asked for it."

It seemed as if a demon was inside him. He grabbed her. Then he started being cruel in his bid to punish her. She screamed with pain. When she tried to shake him off, he hit her hard. She tried to hit him back but he was too strong for her. She could not bear it.

She yanked herself out of his reach and ran outside. She was mindless with fear. The only thing that she could think of was, that she should be as far as possible from Daman and soon she found herself in front of Heera's room, banging the door with all her might.

The moment Heera opened the door, Aina was in his arms crying her heart out. He pulled her inside and held her after shutting the door. He let her cry, caressing her head gently. When her sobs subsided, he pulled away and gasped as he saw Aina.

Aina's face and neck were swollen. Her clothes were torn and he could see the scratches and bruises on her delicate skin. He pulled her to him again and she winced. He hated Daman at that moment.

"I will kill that bastard," he said through gritted teeth as he gently led her to sit down on his bed. She flinched as she saw the bed, but he said, "Don't be afraid of me. I will never take unfair advantage of you.

I will never hurt you Aina. Come and relax with a free mind."

He then put ointment on her bruises. As he finished she said, "Heera, are all husbands cruel? Does every woman suffer like this? Have I done the wrong thing by running away?"

"No Aina. You did the right thing. Nearly all men may be possessive and jealous, but they should be gentle too. Unfortunately you have been married to the wrong man. I often think that he is a gay," said Heera.

"I have been born with a bad destiny. Swami Ram said that it was my destiny to suffer," said Aina.

"I differ from your Swami Ram. Maybe your getting married to Daman was a plan of destiny, but it is in your hands whether you want to tolerate it or not? Aren't you being too submissive?" asked Heera.

Aina said, "Today I was defying them, that is why Daman was so cruel. Till now I was submissive because my parents expect this of me. It was drilled into me. I always wanted to live life on my own terms but before my wedding, my mother made me swear on her head that I would be subservient to my husband always. I thought that I have to accept my destiny and make this marriage work. If I don't, she may die. I won't be able to bear it if something happens to my mother."

"Do you want to go away back to your house, Aina? I can take you there," offered Heera.

"I am sure that my mother will send me back here by the next train. I have to adjust here somehow. But Daman is very cruel. Still I will defy them again, but my mother will be very angry when she comes to know."

Heera said, "I think that your mother would not have been able to see you suffer like this. She couldn't be having any idea that you are going through this trauma because of her. If she knew, probably she would be the first person to tell you to get out of this situation as fast as you can."

"I never thought about that. You may be right," said Aina.

Suddenly there was a banging on the door. Heera opened the door and both Suryakumari and Ram Katori came in, spitting fury at him, "How dare you be in the same room as my daughter-in-law."

Ram Katori went on ranting and Heera kept quiet. When she had exhausted herself, he said, "Madam. Please stop your tirade and wait for fifteen minutes. I am going to call the police."

"The police! Why?" screamed Ram Katori.

"Look at your daughter-in-law. She has been mauled by your son," said Heera.

"Don't blame my son. You must have done it," said Ram Katori.

"Fine. You tell the police that I have done this, but first let me go and get the police," said Heera.

Suryakumari said, "A husband can do what he wants with his wife. Who are you to intrude?"

"Explain all this to the police, Madam. Just let me go to get the police," said Heera.

Ram Katori said, "No. You will not go to the police."

"Then give your daughter-in-law another room just now, this minute. I will not let her stay with that brute of a son of yours," said Heera.

"All right," said Ram Katori, submissively.

Heera made Aina sit in his room till Aina's stuff was shifted to another room. Then Heera took her to that room and said, "Bolt the door from inside whenever you are in the room and don't open the door for Daman."

"All right. Thank you," whispered Aina.

Heera replied, "Try not to let them traumatize you and remember that I keep my promises and from now on, your happiness is my responsibility. I will try to stop them from hurting you, but you have to stand up for yourself. I am sure your mother would say the same thing if she knew how much you are suffering. You have to make your life better. I know that you can do it."

A steely look came into her usually soft eyes and she murmured, "Yes, I won't take it any longer."

Heera walked away with a heavy heart, knowing how difficult it would be for Aina to assert herself under the circumstances, but the arrow had made its mark on Aina, with the hope that maybe her mother also would want her to rebel, given the terrible circumstances.

That day Heera saw to it that in her room Aina got something to eat. Heera told the old servant Girdhari, "Give her regular meals and if Madam tells you not to, then tell me. I will talk to Madam. I don't know why she is being so cruel to her daughter-in-law."

Girdhari had sympathy for Aina because he knew how selfish and ruthless both Ram Katori and Daman were, so he saw to it that Aina got food to eat. From that day Aina stayed in her room and she did not come out. So she did not come face to face with Daman or his mother, and she could rest in complete peace.

After that, often when Ram Katori and Daman would go out, Heera would spend some time with Aina. The servants felt sorry for the new bride and so did not let out about these secret heart-warming meetings. So Daman and Ram Katori never came to know.

Aina and Heera would sit apart and talk. They would not touch each other, because both respected her marriage to Daman, but their eyes devoured each other and their yearning said it all. And they could talk to each other freely and frankly about everything on earth.

They told each other their life stories. Heera told her that his parents had died. His mother had died when he was a child. His father Mohanlal had been friends with Daman's father. He was greatly respected and, on his death bed, he had asked Heera to continue working in that household till he was comfortable with it, because he had strong links with this family.

He said, "So I am still here, though my father has passed away. I don't have any siblings or any relatives who miss me much. So I am quite a free bird. I don't feel any hesitation in telling you that I really don't like the people of this house. Both Daman and his mother are very selfish, greedy and ruthless. You are gentle and nice, so you are a total misfit here."

Aina found herself telling him her innermost secrets. She told him about Baba. About her nightmares. About a person following her when she could hear his breathing. How it had finally stopped.

Heera would listen, believe, understand and empathise. He would comfort her, console her and reassure her. Just like she had always wanted. Her heart told her that Heera was her soulmate. Now she felt that she could never live without Heera. He was her lifeline.

Now she told Heera, "I can bear anything because I have your support."

Heera said, "I am always there for you, Aina, but I can't bear to see you suffer. It cuts me up and hurts me when I see you in pain. Please take care of yourself. You are very precious to me. I can't see you crying."

"Really? Why?" asked Aina.

Heera said, "I don't know if it is the right thing or not, but you have started meaning a lot to me. I just wait for an opportunity to come and talk to you. I can't live without meeting you. It is the wrong thing to do as you are married, but I cannot help myself any more. I need you and love you. If only you were unmarried, I would have made you mine as soon as I could."

He said it seriously and to her it seemed the natural thing to reply, "And I would have loved to be yours." Aina felt that life was becoming more tolerable because she had Heera in the house as a support.

And one day, Heera came to her room again and said, "Both Daman and his mother have gone out, so you can come out of your room. But I want to spend some time with you. It is hell not being able to see you."

Aina kept sitting. On seeing Heera, she too had realized how much she had missed him. She admitted, "I would much rather stay here and spend time with you."

Suddenly Heera walked up to her and stood before her, putting his hand under her chin and tilting her head back. He said, "Don't move. Wait. Your thoughts see me through the time I spend away from you. So let me just see your beauty and memorise it. But I think it is not a good idea because I feel like crushing you to me."

"Yes and that would be wrong," said Aina softly, and then Heera sat away from her and they just talked.

CHAPTER 24

After a few days, Girdhari came and said to Aina, "Daman Sahab wants you to know that your father is coming tomorrow to take you home. He says you can take all your belongings and stay in your mother's house forever. He has said that you should not come back."

Aina was left with mixed feelings. She was happy that she was going away from the hell of her in-law's house. But she was feeling extremely sad too, and she realised that this sadness was because there was no certainty that she would ever meet her Heera again. Suddenly Aina could not imagine a life without Heera.

She felt so upset, that she forgot everything and ran to Heera's room. She reached his room and sobbed, "Heera. My father is coming to take me home tomorrow. Daman does not want me to come back here. I am going away for ever. Oh Heera! How will I live without you?"

"Aina! No. I don't want you to go away from me. Please marry me. I can't live without you either. Now I just live for you, my darling. I know that I will miss you."

Aina said, "Heera I will miss you too, but how can I marry you? My life is a mess. I think you should find a woman who is single and without problems."

And Aina began to cry uncontrollably.

"Aina, please don't cry. I have thought about it very seriously. I need you, at any cost. Please don't ever doubt me on that. I am always here for you. I love you."

"I know that. I love you too Heera. I don't want to leave you ever. Oh! I feel so helpless," sobbed Aina.

Heera took her in his arms. Gently he caressed her hair and face, and said, "Aina, I yearn for you. How will I live without you? I don't want to live a single minute without you. I want you. I need you so much. Stay with me always. We will go far away somewhere else."

Aina felt shy to say anything more. How could she tell him that she found it so nice to touch him and also that she loved every touch of his? Till now she had thought that the touch of every man would be repugnant to her, but his touch was so soothing that it filled up the gnawing vacuum in her heart. How could she tell him that he made her feel happy and needed, as never before? He was like her very heart beat and breath.

Aloud Aina said, "Heera, you are not like other men. You have given me the faith that men can be good also. It is not certain that we will meet again. If we can't meet, the memory of being with you will be enough to see me through a lifetime. But now I must go. I don't want to have any one see me here. It would spoil our reputations. You will get into trouble. You may lose your job. Let me go. Someone may come. Good bye, Heera."

Heera stubbornly said, "No. It isn't 'Good bye'. We will always be together." And he caught her fiercely and rained kisses on her face, whispering, "Oh! My darling! My heart beat. I can live a whole lifetime for you. I can die for you. Don't leave me alone, my dearest."

His passion ignited her mind and body till she matched the strength of his ardour. Then with a desperate passion he loved her and she responded. He told her that he adored her young body as well as her kind heart and told her all she meant to him. Aina clutched him with all her body and soul. Every cell and pore of her radiant body felt awake, pulsating with carefree ecstasy. For the first time she felt wonderful sensations coursing through her. Then both of them forgot everything. No one else existed except their love for each other. They felt pure bliss and she came to know what happiness and fulfilment were.

Later they lay there cuddled in each other's arms, forgetting the issues that troubled them. They forgot society, ethics and their inbuilt inhibitions in their sublime contentment of being with each other. They were loathe to think of even a moment without the other.

Aina's spirit soared, as her heart sang, because she felt so loved. Her neglected and ignored soul now revelled in his attention. And she did not feel guilty. The new sensations that she had experienced were mind boggling for her. She was now smitten with Heera. His love gave her anchorage, and the courage to face life.

Heera said, "Aina, get away from this marriage and marry me. I will live just to make you happy. I love you so much that it pains me to be away from you."

Aina replied, "I love you too Heera but it is not so simple. I have two families to think of. Daman behaves funnily with me, I still don't know why he married me, but the fact remains that I am married to him. I can marry you only by leaving him through a divorce and that would kill my parents. Moreover a divorce would tarnish his image, so Daman will not be ready for it."

Aina and Heera talked and seemed to come back to the same thing, the futility of their love which could not culminate in the fruition of marriage. Now they were reluctant to leave each other because they did not know if they would ever meet again, and this very fact frightened them. Aina forced herself to move away from him, still tingling from his touch; and then she went to her room, agony and ecstasy fighting a duel inside her.

The next day Aina came out of her room only when Girdhari told her that her father had arrived. When she saw her father, she was shocked. Her father Kalka had become very thin and he looked defeated by life.

Kalka said, "I have come personally to invite your family for three weddings. Girish, Sabal and Prabal are getting married. Rukmini Chachi has insisted that you should come for the weddings. You have to come. She will feel hurt if you don't come along with me."

Aina was happy to hear the news that her uncles were getting married. She respected Rukmini and felt sympathy for her on account of the Sudha bua episode. So she felt she must go to attend the weddings. She replied, "Yes, Papa, I will certainly accompany you."

He said, "Aina. I hope they are not ill treating you. We had received a letter from Daman that he wanted us to give him money for setting up a business."

Aina could not believe it because she knew that Daman had plenty of money.

She said, "Papa, he has lots of money. These people are greedy. That is why they have demanded money. I hope you did not give the money to him."

He said, "Frankly Aina, we don't have the money to give. So I sent a letter refusing him. I also told him that I would come today to fetch you home."

Aina thought about the fact that Daman had not told her about the money. This must be a sort of a planned move. She felt afraid, but she did not let her father know about the situation as she understood why Daman had asked for money. Daman wanted her to go away and leave him. That is why he had asked for dowry, because he knew that her parents would not be able to give a dowry because of their low finances.

Her father had brought a lot of sweets and dry fruits, but Ram Katori felt that Aina's father had not brought enough and she refused to take anything.

She shouted at Aina's father, "You come here without bringing clothes for me and my son. If you are a pauper and could not give money, then atleast you should have brought some big gift for my son. And what have you taught your daughter? She is very rude and impudent. You have not taught her good values and decency. But whatever, she is my daughter-in-law. I will not let Aina go. And before going, you must tell your daughter to behave well and look after everyone here."

"My cousin brothers are getting married. All the daughters of the family are coming for these weddings. Aina hasn't come to our place even once after her wedding. Please allow her to come. I have come to personally invite you all to come to Najapur for the wedding," pleaded Kalka, trying to appease her.

"You really think I will go to your poverty stricken house for the wedding? Even my son will not go there."

Aina felt very bad for her father as Ram Katori was very rude. Aina hated to see her father plead with her mother-in-law. She started feeling very angry but she knew that if she said anything to her mother-in-law, her father would be the first person to scold her.

At that time Daman was not in the house. Aina asked her father to stay there till Daman came. It was a punishment because her father had to remain hungry for all that time, because a girl's relative was not supposed to eat or drink at her in-law's place. Finally they heard Daman coming. Aina opened the front door.

Before he could enter, Aina said to Daman, "My father has come to fetch me for the weddings of his cousin brothers, but your mother is not letting me go. I find that surprising because you want me to go forever and I also want to go. So you must persuade her to let me go, otherwise I will tell my father how much you and your mother have troubled me. My Sabal chacha is a lawyer. He can take you to court for domestic violence."

As Daman came in, his mother started ranting at Aina and her father, but for once Daman was firm and said to Ram Katori, "No Mataji. Aina will go to her father's place for the three weddings."

Aina understood that he had taken this stance so readily because he had wanted her to go away and leave him. Ram Katori was left speechless, and in a huff she said, "Do what you want, but I will not give a paisa of your father's property to you." This upset Daman.

Ram Katori went away sulking to her room but Daman went after her to appease her. Then he came out and said to Aina, "My mother is very upset. She does not want you to go to your parent's house. So tell your father that you will not go. Couldn't he have brought some money or gifts? What selfish, miserly and stupid parents you have, who don't want their daughter's happiness."

A blinding fury caught Aina. She shouted, "Don't you dare say a word against my parents."

She grabbed the surprised Daman's hand and pulled him into his mother's room. Ram Katori was sulking. She was sitting on the bed with her back towards the door and she wouldn't look at Aina. Then through gritted teeth Aina said, "Listen you both. I will go home with my father and you both can not stop me."

Ram Katori said, "Daman see how rude your wife is."

Before Daman could speak, Aina said, "I am not as rude as you were to my father. Let me go or I will tell everyone what a brute your son is."

Ram Katori said, "Go tell the world. I will tell them that Heera did this to you."

Aina said, "You are the devil incarnate. If you don't let me go, I will tell the world whose son Daman is. Those who have skeletons in their cupboards should keep quiet. Be afraid that your secrets may get out."

Daman seemed shocked and said, "What a silly thing to say. I am my parent's son."

Aina said, "No. Think why your mother is quiet! Daman you are not the child of your father. Your father and uncle did not want normal sex. Your father was impotent and his younger brother was frigid, so they had no heirs. Someone else was called by your father to get your mother pregnant and then you were born."

Daman raised his hand to hit Aina, but she caught his hand and said, "Look at your mother and then ask her if I am speaking the truth or not."

Ram Katori was sitting pale and drained. She said nothing at all. Aina had never seen her so shaken.

Daman looked at his mother and said, "Mataji. Why don't you say that Aina is wrong?"

But it seemed as if Ram Katori had become dumb. Then Aina said, "I could have used this secret information to blackmail both of you since the beginning, but I thought that my parents would want me to compromise with my husband and in-laws to sustain our marriage. You are ranting against those same parents whom I adore. So now I refuse to compromise at all. The moment you trouble me, I will tell everyone this secret. Don't try my patience any more. Be careful from this moment. Now I am going with my father and both of you better be civil to my father and to me."

Aina left Daman staring at his mother. Aina went to her room and picked up her suitcase. As she came out of her room, she banged into Heera.

"Are you going now Aina?" he asked.

"Yes. My father has come. Mataji insulted my father. She made him beg and plead. I hate her. I never want to come back to this house," said Aina.

"I understand. She and Daman have become obnoxious. You are doing the right thing. Rather I am glad that you are doing something to save yourself. If you are going, then I will also leave this place. The moment I get a job somewhere else, I will come to you."

Aina said, "Somehow Heera, I am feeling that by going, I am playing into the hands of Daman. I feel that he wants me to go. But he is such a rogue that even this realisation does not make me prepared to stay back here. This house has been a hell for me. I have to go."

"Yes, you must go. These people will hurt you if you don't go now," said Heera.

"Good bye Heera," said Aina.

"Goodbye Aina."

As she was walking off, she felt like crying and she realized it was because of Heera. She did not want to leave him. Rather she wanted to rush back to him and hold him and never leave him. She dragged her feet forward. She should do the correct thing.

However, he called her name, then rushed to her and held her tight as if he would never leave her.

He said, "Aina. Leave that scoundrel Daman. He doesn't deserve you. It is hurting me to see you go away from me. This cannot be goodbye. We are meant for each other. We will meet again, I promise."

"I believe you, I love you," said Aina.

"You can trust me Aina, I love you too," said Heera.

She heard her father calling. She looked at Heera for the last time and sobbing, ran away from him.

She heard Heera shout, "We will meet again Aina. I will wait for you. I will marry you, I promise."

Aina left the house with her father. Throughout the journey, her father kept sobbing, "I am sorry Aina that we married you to Daman. I can see that you are suffering. I am sorry that I didn't put my foot down to stop your wedding. I feel so guilty. I have been a bad and selfish father. Aina! Please forgive me."

She tried her best to console him. As they neared the palace, Aina thought, "Will Ma be loving towards me?" Then they reached home and Aina saw her mother. She was shocked to see her. She had become weak and looked quite old. They held each other and cried out their misery.

Aina gasped, "Ma I will not go back. See these marks. He has hurt me. I can't go back to him."

Her mother was scandalized. She stopped crying at once and said sternly, "Don't talk like this Aina. Husbands can do what they want. When a girl is married, she has to be true to her husband throughout her life. She has to be there with him till her death. You can't leave him. A bride should go after marriage to her husband's house and only her dead body should leave it. See I never left your father despite everything that I suffered in this house. I have stuck it out with him."

Aina pleaded, "Ma, you don't know. Daman behaves with me like a demon. He hurts me."

"Stop. That is between you and your husband. You should not be telling me," said her mother.

Aina felt trapped. She knew that she wouldn't be given freedom from Daman. Her parents and her relatives would insist on her going back to Daman.

She thought, "What should I do? I feel so good away from that house. The only one I miss is Heera. Oh Heera! I love you so much. I cannot live without you."

Her mother patted her and said without knowing what Aina was thinking, "Everything will be all right. Forget yourself and concentrate on the weddings."

Aina took her cue from that. She remembered that her Baba had said, 'Just celebrate life'. She tried to forget the problems in her own life and she just tried to take happiness from being near her parents.

Thankfully Sonali had also gone to her father's house, so the house was peaceful. Moreover she got a chance to meet Bela and Veena Amma. The best thing was that she met Rukmini Amma. Even Prasad Baba was not as strict as he used to be. Age and ill health had mellowed him down. Girish was talkative now. He was marrying a girl from his office and now he was happy.

Aina was happy that Rukmini had decided to have the three weddings from the ancestral palace. It seemed like a homecoming for them too. Now Prasad and Rukmini were the eldest in the family and Gomti discussed Aina's refusal to go to her in-law's house.

They kept quiet and then Rukmini said, "Aina. You enjoy the weddings. Afterwards we will talk about this, but whatever happens, we want your happiness."

So Aina delved into the festivities trying to recapture the artless innocence that had allowed her to experience happiness in earlier times. Unfortunately, with happiness, the pain also would hit her as strongly, because her Baba was not there and everything had changed for the worse. It hurt her the most, that despite the perfect rapport they always had, Baba had died when she had been angry with him because of Sudha bua. Like her, he must have been hurt by her anger. She wished that she was not so sensitive, then life would be far better. So she tried not to think, but just to enjoy.

CHAPTER 25

The weddings were celebrated in a very grand manner. For Aina it was a lovely wedding Reception to remember because there was such a lot of change in the old claustrophobic traditions. Girish, Sabal and Prabal were marrying girls of their own choice, because after the tragedy of Sudha, Rukmini always wanted her sons to be free to do things that would give them happiness.

She did not bother about what society would say and somehow Prasad would listen to her, because now he seemed to have lost his rigid stance. He appeared old, lost and aimless; now more amiable and less stern.

Aina was also thrilled to see the changes in the social conditions, specially in the status of women. Now women came out in front of the men and that also without a veil on their heads. Society was becoming modern and women were studying and doing jobs.

Aina was very happy to see that all the three brides were educated and of a good temperament. Aina was sure that the new brides would look after Rukmini Amma and Prasad Baba. Atleast they were not like Sonali, who had continued her selfishness by not coming for the weddings. Not that anybody minded.

But some customs continued. The eunuchs came as usual, to congratulate the newly weds, but Laila was not with them. Aina recognized another old eunuch Chameli and asked him about Laila. Chameli told her that Laila was sick. Aina felt helpless that she couldn't go to meet her own brother. But Aina was aghast as she heard Chameli say, "Laila has given away all his money. There is no one to look after him. He is in a bad state."

"Where did Laila give his money?" asked Aina.

"Didn't you know? They found his family. Laila sent all his savings to his mother. Every month he would send one thousand rupees. Then for a wedding, he sent twenty thousand rupees. What a horrible family he has. No one bothers about him now. Poor Laila!"

Aina opened her purse and gave all the money in it to Chameli. Aina said, "Please give this to Laila and tell him to go to a doctor immediately."

"Oh! You are so generous but just look at his family. They don't even care for Laila just because he is an eunuch, though they kept the money he had sent."

Obviously Chameli did not know who Laila's mother was. Aina kept quiet but then she walked to a secluded corner and she cried out her guilt. Her mother caught her crying and Aina told her that the money had been sent by Laila and not Daman, but her mother would not believe it. Her mother said, "It must have been your Daman who sent the money. Have you asked Daman?"

Aina said, "No Ma, but he isn't the type to give money to anyone. He gives me money just because he thinks that he gets power over me. He feels that he can control me in this way because I am from a poor family. He must have found out that though we are a reputed family, our finances are not so good. That is why he asked for my hand, thinking that as I am from a poor household, I would always obey them. You don't know him. He is very calculating and manipulative."

"Now forget your life and enjoy the Reception," said her mother and Aina did just that.

Slowly the busy atmosphere slowed down after the celebrations were over. On the last day when the bridegrooms were taking their brides to their house in Lucknow, a mystery got solved for Aina, one that had been pursuing her since her childhood.

Aina tripped and was falling when Girish caught her and held her till she regained her balance. Girish had fear in his eyes, as probably he was afraid that she may recognize his touch. And that is exactly what happened. Aina realized by his touch and his rasping asthmatic breathing, that he was her childhood tormentor. She straightened and looked him straight in the eye. She said angrily, "So, you are the one who was after me. Do you know what I suffered? You gave me hell at a time when I was the most vulnerable. Why did you do it?"

"I did it to take revenge from your Mahavir Baba. He did not let me marry my beloved," said Girish.

"And what about my life? Should I now go and tell your bride-to-be about you?" asked Aina.

Girish looked cornered and he begged, "No Aina. Let bygones be bygones. Please don't tell anyone. I am sorry for what I did. Forget everything and I promise I will never trouble you any more."

"One apology will not wash away the fears and tears that you made me suffer," and she raised her right hand and gave Girish a tight slap on the right cheek and then on the left cheek. She tripped him when he was least expecting it and he sprawled on the floor. Then she kicked him hard and he screamed because of the pain.

She shouted at him, "You had wanted to hurt me. Now I will hurt you."

She was about to kick him again when she saw a laughing Rukmini and a smiling Prasad coming that way, and she stopped. She did not want to disrupt their happiness. They did not deserve her revenge.

Girish pleaded, "What I did was unpardonable Aina and I shouldn't have done it. Please forgive me."

For the sake of his parents, she forgave Girish. Aina thus buried the trauma of her childhood.

But other things bothered her too. She felt bad when she saw that the initial large family appeared to have suffered a lot of wear and tear. The whole palace and the compound had become congested as there were cemented jail-like buildings everywhere. There were court cases on between various family members over the boundaries of their property within the palace.

She was shocked also at the state her parents were in. Munna had gone to stay in the ancestral house of his wife Sonali's parents for good. Munna was living now with his father-in-law and managing his business. He did not send any money home. When Gomti tried to contact her, Sonali made it very clear that she did not want any contact with Munna's family. Munna just said, "You married me to this girl. I am helpless. But don't sell your portion. I have the sole right to your property."

Munna did not care for his mother who felt wounded at the turn of her own most loved son against her. Munna did not know what a deep scar he had left on his mother's heart. She gave up her will to live from that day, because Munna had always been her favourite child. Aina told her parents to throw Munna out of their lives and they promised that they would. Moreover Aina could not bear to see that there was no money in the house for her mother's medicines, as her parents had debts and they were suffering from financial problems.

She knew that her husband Daman would refuse to help her family. Now she took out enough cash for her return ticket to Rojpur, just in case she was sent back by her mother to her in-law's house, and she gave the rest of the money to her father. She also gave her jewellery to her mother to sell when the money finished. As she was still accountable for the jewellery to Daman and Ram Katori, she decided to tell them that she had been robbed of her jewellery in the train on her return.

Aina said, "Ma, I will send money to you every month."

Her mother burst out crying. Her father said, "No Aina you should not think of sending money. I am trying to get a job soon and everything will be all right."

Then the day came when her mother told her to go back, but she dreaded going back. She could not stop herself and she blurted everything to Rukmini.

Rukmini said firmly, "Aina will not go to that house ever." She made Prasad send a letter to Daman that he would not send Aina back, because she had been exploited in his house.

His mother Ram Katori's reply came, "Aina has a problem with me, not with Daman. I will live alone in this present house, while Aina and Daman can stay on in another new house that we own. Heera is getting the new house ready. Aina can go straight to her new house and never meet me. I will not interfere in their marital life. So, Aina should be sent to stay with Daman."

Her mother now forced Aina to go. Aina tried her best to make her mother understand. She said, "Ma.

The problem is not only my mother-in-law. I hate being with Daman alone in the night."

"And I told you that you should not discuss all this outside your bedroom. If you don't go, can you imagine what shame will befall this family? How will we face society?" said her mother.

"Ma, you are always bothered about society. Doesn't it matter to you that I am suffering and will suffer more if sent there. They can burn me or murder me in some way," said Aina.

"If you don't go there, then what will you do?" asked her mother.

"Ma I will file for a divorce," said Aina.

"Just shut up. Divorce! In my family! Never! You have to go back to Daman," screamed Gomti.

"You don't care for me, Ma. You really are very hardhearted and selfish. You could not be loving even towards Laila and now you are throwing me again into a burning furnace," said Aina.

Still Gomti had her way in the end and it was also because Aina let herself be persuaded. Her mother-in-law Ram Katori's letter had made it clear that Heera was still there. Aina cherished her memories of Heera. She held them close to her heart and she knew that nobody could take away the happiness she had felt. She hated being with Daman, but she loved Heera and so she let herself be persuaded to go back.

A day before Aina had to leave for Rojpur they heard a child shout, "The eunuchs have come." Gomti stiffened but Aina ran outside and saw that a group of eunuchs was singing at the house of a relative. She went closer and saw Laila, her brother, who asked, "How are you sister? I hope everything is all right."

Aina said, "How are you? You were sick, weren't you?"

Laila said, "Yes thank you for the money. I was sick, but I am fine now. How are your parents?"

"Our parents are not all right," said Aina. Then Aina told Laila the condition of their parents.

Laila said, "Don't worry. I will look after them."

Aina said, "You have already done enough for us. Chameli told me that you were sending money to us. I am not worried about our parents because I know that you are here to look after them. Now I have to go back to Rojpur tomorrow, though I am not very happy there."

Laila said, "Take care of yourself. I hope things get better. Don't tell anyone that I sent the money as they would not like it because I am not a normal man."

Aina said, "You are better than any man. Munna has left our parents in the lurch while you cared for them. You are such a wonderful brother to have. I think you are better off being what you are, because I feel that nearly all men are horrible creatures. You take care of yourself. If you need anything, just let me know. Our parents will manage for some time, as I have given them money and my jewellery. I will go on sending money to them."

Laila said, "Just now I don't have money to give, but I will certainly keep tabs on them and help them if they need anything. And if you need anything, just let me know." They exchanged addresses and then they said good bye, not knowing if they would meet again.

The next day she had packed and was ready to go to Rojpur. Though she was desirous to be with Heera, Aina cried because now she would have to be with her husband Daman also. She had a very strong antipathy for Daman which made her dread seeing him again. Her Sabal chacha was sent to escort her. When Daman came to receive her at the station, he too did not seem too enchanted to see Aina. Sabal went back to Najapur with a lot of misgivings. He couldn't forget how Aina had clung to him desperately and said in such a pitiable way, "I wish I didn't have to come back here."

Sabal went to Gomti and said, "Aina told me everything. Aina has enough grounds to get a divorce. I can file a suit against Daman whenever you say."

But because of the family's prestige, Gomti did not want Aina to come back home. She shouted, "Sabal, don't you dare get Aina a divorce. I will never talk to you if you do. A girl should only stay in her in-law's house."

Sabal cried that night alone in his room. He didn't know what he was crying for. Was he crying for Aina or Sudha or all the women who had to suffer so much? He made up his mind to look after his bride very well. Professionally, as a lawyer, he decided that he would take up and fight the cases of exploited women, beginning with Aina, if she ever decided to get a divorce.

CHAPTER 26

Aina reached her in-law's new house in which she was supposed to live now with Daman. It was a huge, palatial house. Aina followed Daman into a spacious room. She liked it. It was beautifully decorated and furnished. Daman sent his old servant Girdhari to get her suitcase and dispassionately said to her, "This is your bedroom. Don't come out of it. Stay out of my life also. Mataji is at our old house and will not interfere."

Aina kept quiet. A maid servant brought all her meals to Aina's room. Aina was quite relieved when she came to know that Daman had seen to it also that he and Aina had separate bedrooms, but the question was, would he stay away from her? She knew that still she wouldn't be able to suffer any intimacy with him.

She thought, "Daman is keeping his distance from me, so what can be the reason that he agreed to call me here?" She soon analysed the reason. Ram Katori was the heir to her husband's will and it would be in her hands whether Daman would get the wealth and property. So he must be obeying her. But why should he shun her? Did he love some other girl? Was he gay? But then why did he marry her? She suddenly thought, "But where is Heera? I haven't seen him at all. Has he left his job here? Oh Heera! Come to me. I wish my marriage ends and I can marry you. I wish I can get a divorce."

But she had seen how her own mother had baulked at the idea of a divorce; probably Ram Katori would have a similar misgiving against her son giving a divorce to Aina. What a cul de sac her life had reached!

"Oh Lord! What will happen now? Will I live my life like this? Will I never be able to marry Heera? Oh Lord! Help me." She was also very tense that Daman might maul her again.

As she lay with her eyes wide open, she heard a noise outside. "Is it Daman? Oh my God! I haven't bolted the door." She rushed to the door noiselessly to slip the bolt in. Then she stopped. She had heard voices. She peeped outside. She saw Daman seeing off someone. In a low voice, Daman had said, "You must come to me tomorrow. Be careful. Now Mataji has called that woman back. I don't want her to find out. She may trouble us."

There had been an affirmative "Hmmm, as you say. I will come if you want me to, but I need money."

"You will get it. Meet me in my study here tomorrow evening at six," answered Daman. Then Daman had closed the door, turned and gone away to his bedroom without even glancing at her room. Whose voice had that been? She had heard that voice somewhere. She must find out. What money were they talking about? There was something really fishy going on. But atleast Daman was not intruding on her. She heaved a sigh of relief and lay down to sleep.

The next day she was served her meals in her room again. She spent part of the day walking through the big house. She entered a room which was full of books. Now she would have something to do. She happily picked up a book to read.

At six in the evening, the doorbell rang. She realized that one visitor had come in and he had been taken to the study by Daman. Aina waited for five minutes and then she went into the study. She covered her head. She knocked and in a trice opened the door herself and entered. She saw that Daman was with a young man. On seeing her there, Daman and the young man looked more nervous than she was.

The young man was sitting in front of Daman and there was a briefcase open on the study table and the young man was counting money.

Daman's face showed his guilt, but then anger took over as he said, "Why have you come here? What is the matter? Go to your room at once."

Aina took two deep breaths and said, "I thought some guests have come, so I came to ask if you wanted me to make tea for them. Good evening. I am his wife. Do you want a cup of tea?" she asked the visitor.

The man did not know how to react, but Daman said, "No. You can go. He wants nothing."

Aina went to her bedroom and thought, "What is going on? There was a lot of money in that briefcase. And why had they looked so guilty if this was from a legal business? It seems they are doing some illegal business. Or is that man blackmailing Daman? Or is Daman a homosexual as Heera suspects? Could that man be his gay partner? I must find out the truth about Daman and his relationship with that visitor."

She knew that she would be punished for her intrusion, by Daman in some way and she prepared herself for it. Half an hour later the old trusted servant Girdhari knocked at her door which she had bolted from inside and told her that Daman was calling her.

She went to the study where there was no sign of the money transaction. The young man also had gone.

Daman didn't even tell her to sit. He just said, "From now on you will never come inside my study till I call you. You can just stay in your bedroom."

"Why? Are you doing some illegal or immoral thing? Are you being blackmailed?" asked Aina boldly.

Daman rushed towards her, ready to hit her.

Aina replied, "Don't you dare hit me. I will not take any nonsense anymore. I know your secret."

Daman stopped in his tracks. He said, "Shut up. I am a businessman, so these transactions are normal. They are legal. I am also going to stand for an election. So I don't want you to create any problem. You are my wife, because my mother wants this farce to continue. I would end this marriage just now, if left to me."

Aina looked contemptuously at him and said, "I will remain your wife on one condition. Write your full property in my name and put money in my bank so that I don't have to come to your study to ask for money. And I want this done today, so that I don't have to depend on you ever again, or come to your study like a beggar."

"How dare you! Why should I give my property to you?"

"Because I have a secret about your birth up my sleeve."

"I can't give everything to you. All this is my mother's property."

"Then give me an allowance from what you have. I can call Heera and ask him the details."

"No, you don't call him. I will get the papers made."

Aina sat down on a chair and did not budge from there till Daman had called his lawyer and told him to draw up the papers. Within two days the papers had been signed, a new bank account opened in Aina's name and money deposited to the tune of one lac.

Aina felt good about having this substantial money. She felt secure and she was now self sufficient for some time, atleast where money was concerned.

She became fully relieved that Daman would never come to her in the night because she realized that Daman was very busy with planning to stand for the elections to the State Assembly next year. His secretary Rocoo was helping him in his business and politics.

Rocoo was short, fat and very haughty. He just avoided Aina and he didn't acknowledge her presence at all, which Aina found very insulting. But she realized that the voice in the night at the front door had not been Rocoo's. Girdhari, the old servant, told her that Daman mostly spent time with Manav, who stayed in the same city, in a house nearby, and who was a trader. Somehow Aina had never got to meet Manav.

Now Aina felt bored at home. There was Girdhari and a maidservant to do the housework, so Aina planned to explore the city herself, but at first she felt nervous to venture out alone. She set her mind on becoming a self sufficient and fearless individual. She reminded herself, 'I am brave. I depend on myself only. I smile always.' She forced herself to go out alone despite her fears. Daman would take his new Ambassador car to his office, so she would travel by local transport.

Aina felt amazed by the quaint town of Rojpur. There was an airfield near by and she loved seeing the aeroplanes fly past. The best part was she felt free and she started enjoying herself. She had money, and she roamed the markets and bought books for herself. Tired, she would return and then she educated herself by reading voraciously. Her awareness of the world increased and she realized how free women could be.

They were very confident and could live life on their own terms. She imbibed and absorbed the realities of life. She thought about her life. She realized that Heera's surmise might be correct that Daman was a homosexual and that Manav was the gay partner of Daman. She wanted to meet Manav so that she could see for herself if these deductions were correct. She tried to piece together the jigsaw puzzle that would help her life to be free of the knots that had tied her so irrevocably to a scoundrel. She had no objection to his being a gay, but she did not like his spoiling her life.

Why did he marry her at all? If he had a gay tendency, he could have been bravely honest about it and not ruined her life in the bargain.

She also read about how divorce was becoming common in society though women divorcees were still looked down upon. But whenever she thought of taking a divorce from her husband, she remembered her own mother's parting words to her, "Aina. You have to make this marriage work, otherwise you will see my dead face, as there will be disgrace for us and nothing else."

Though Aina felt that she was no longer bound by her mother's words, guilt suffused her. Her mother had been shocked when she had merely spoken the word divorce. Taking a divorce would create havoc.

Then she thought, "I will not take an emotional decision. Let me take time and think objectively."

It was very difficult because she had been so protected always, but when Daman left her alone, slowly she was able to gather courage and manage alone so that she learnt to be independent. Moreover she saw that she had the potential of making her own choices and the grit to stand up for her own convictions.

Her attitude to life changed. She now felt bold enough to take her own decisions and be prepared to face the consequences courageously. She no longer got panic attacks and she stopped fearing everything and everyone. She even lost her fear of Daman, specially as she realized that Daman was now more vulnerable, as he needed her to be with him for a spotless reputation.

She became friendly with her neighbours and she would often go to their houses to spend time with them. She made a friend and invited her home. That day Daman asked her, "Why did you bring this girl home?"

"This girl works for a newspaper. I can get you free publicity for your election. I can also get the details of your birth published whenever you want," said Aina.

"Shut up and I don't want that girl coming here into my house," shouted Daman.

"And I am not going to obey you," retorted Aina.

CHAPTER 27

As he was busy planning his strategy for the elections next year, Daman left her alone, till a rumour started gaining prominence that Daman was gay. Now he started feeling that it was a requisite that he should take his wife with him for all the parties and meetings; to negate the rumour and add to his respectability.

He was even invited with his wife as chief guest to various functions and there he had to take Aina. The hesitant Aina refused to go to the first party, but Daman forced her to go. After that Aina was ready to go for parties, but Daman resisted, because it had been an eyeopener for Daman. Aina was a success at the party.

As she had seen the latest trends from the magazines, she had groomed herself well. She had the money to buy stylish clothes though she still covered herself demurely. Now she looked really attractive and charming. She was a good conversationalist and soon she had many admirers. Daman felt jealous when his friends praised Aina and stood around her, listening to her witty repartees and applauding them.

With new eyes Daman looked at Aina. In her multi hued, graceful chiffon saris, with her long open hair and sharp features on her beguiling complexion, she looked captivating. She was still slim, but with curves at the right places. Daman felt jealous of her popularity. One night on his return from the party, he scolded Aina for being too familiar with others. She shouted back at him to mind his own business. After that he only took her to parties where he could not avoid taking her.

One day when there was no one at home, the doorbell rang. Aina opened the front door. She saw the same young man that she had seen counting money with Daman when she had barged into the study.

The man stood there in total silence, and then he said, "You are really beautiful." Then Aina realised that she had forgotten to cover her head. She also remembered that she had heard this voice before. He had been present at their wedding, but they had not seen each other. This man was Manav.

He knew of her just as a nondescript girl from a poor family who obeyed her mother-in-law, sat with a veil on her head and cried a lot. Even on the day that Manav had been with Daman with a lot of money, Aina's face had not been visible because of her veil.

Aina found his way of talking very audacious but when he said, "I am Manav," it confirmed her suspicion that this was the voice she had heard talking to Daman at the front door. Now she moved away to let him come inside. Soon Daman and Rocoo came back too and Aina retired to her room. But Aina had instinctively sensed that the normally suspicious Daman had faith in Manav as if there was a sort of bond between them. She now wanted to find out more. She also felt that Manav had something to hide and she wanted to know what it was.

Daman took her to one party where Manav had also come. Manav was standing near Aina, when a lady came and asked bluntly, "Who is this beauty?"

Manav said, "She is Aina, Daman's wife."

The lady's eyebrows arched unbelievingly and she said softly, "Does Daman accept you with her?"

She heard Manav whisper sharply, "Mind your own business and get lost."

The lady smiled coldly, saying, "Aina, this man is not a woman's man. Beware of him. Bye."

When the lady walked away, Aina asked, "What did she mean?"

Manav said, "Oh! Forget her."

Aina became very curious to know more about Manav.

The next day, as soon as Daman had gone to his office, Heera came to meet Aina.

"Where were you all these days Heera?" cried Aina running into his arms.

"I am sorry Aina but I was busy. I had been told by Madam that I could continue with my job, but I could not stay any longer in the old house. So I have bought a house quite near this new house and I am also looking for another job as I don't want to depend on Daman."

Aina knew that the servants were in the house. She said, "I think, Heera, you better go now."

"I have missed you so much. I love you. What have you thought about us? Can you leave Daman?"

"I love you Heera. I have come back here only because of you. But I am still confused, please give me more time to decide about the divorce," whispered Aina.

Heera said, "Ah! I will wait for that decision."

The next evening Manav came when Daman was not at home. Aina said, "Tell me about Daman."

"What do you want to know about him?"

"Daman has a business and lots of money, so why does he want to stand for an election?"

"I can tell you that. For power, more influence and more wealth. But just now he hasn't got a ticket to stand for the elections. He is trying to get a party ticket."

"Which party does he work for?" asked Aina.

"He works for the Samanya party," answered Manav.

"What if they don't give him a ticket?" asked Aina.

"They will have to give him a ticket. We will see to it that they do," answered Manav in such a menacing tone, that Aina felt that Manav could be dangerous if crossed. She knew that Daman was callous, and both together would be lethal as both Daman and Manav seemed unscrupulous, ruthless and vindictive.

CHAPTER 28

Daman behaved now as if she did not exist. He ignored her completely. She was left alone in the house most of the time. When Daman came home he would usually have either Rocoo or some other person with him. Aina told herself that it was better that Daman spent the day away from her. She felt more relaxed now.

One morning the house reverberated with Daman's anger. Girdhari had dropped a very precious decoration piece and Daman had lost his cool. He ranted savagely at Girdhari and actually hit him.

Girdhari pleaded, "Sahab I have been with your family since you were a baby. If I have dropped just one thing in all these years, do I merit this punishment?"

Daman snarled, "Shut up, you idiot. Don't you dare talk to me like that." Daman picked up his belt and started whipping the poor Girdhari with it.

Then Aina came and held Daman's hand. She shouted, "Don't beat him anymore. He looks after you like a father and this is the respect that you give him. You should be ashamed of yourself."

Daman gave her a withering glance, shook off her hand and walked off. Quickly Aina got the First Aid box because Girdhari's hand was bleeding profusely. She dressed his wound carefully.

Girdhari said, "You are a very nice person. You have a bad destiny that you have been married into this house. You should have got a better husband."

Aina said, "You are also suffering Girdhari."

Girdhari said, "I will not work for him anymore, but before I go I want to tell you a secret. The truth is that Heera is the brother of Daman. Call Heera and tell him to take away all the property of Daman. Heera is such a nice person, while this man Daman is evil."

"But how can you say that Heera is his brother? Can you tell me in detail?" asked Aina.

"Ram Katori had no children because Daman's father could not have children. So Daman is the son of Mohanlal, Heera's father. Mohanlal's wife was very sick. The surgeon asked for a lot of money for her operation. Mohanlal asked Daman's father for the money and the latter said that he would give the money only if he sired a child through Ram Katori. Mohanlal complied just to get the money for his wife's treatment, but unfortunately his wife died, but Daman was born," explained Girdhari.

Aina was quite shocked and Girdhari continued, "That makes Heera and Daman brothers. Tell Heera to file a suit. I will give evidence in the court, but see that Daman is punished," said Girdhari. He then went away after Aina had given him substantial money to take care of himself in his old age. He blessed her from the bottom of his heart and left the house of Daman forever.

Daman had become so busy that he would come late at night or not at all. Aina had always been an insomniac and now alone in the house, Aina would be very afraid. Aina started feeling very depressed because she felt very lonely. One evening, out of boredom, Aina went to the market. When she returned, she opened the front door and stood transfixed. She saw Daman and Manav together in Daman's study. They had guiltily sprung apart from each other. What had they been doing? Aina stared at them and Daman brusquely said, "Where have you been?"

As she stayed quiet, Manav said as if nothing had happened, "How are you, Madam?"

"I will tell you after you have explained what was happening here," said Aina.

Manav said, "Nothing. Daman is upset today. I was just consoling him. I think I must go now."

Aina kept quiet. As soon as Manav went away, Aina confronted Daman, "You are gay."

"So?" asked Daman.

"Why did you marry me?" asked Aina.

Daman said, "Because I needed you as a cover up for my relationships. Because, I had to prove to the world that I am a normal man. Because I need to be known as straight, as a political person should have an untainted reputation. And now that I have proved myself as macho, why don't you just go to your mother's house and leave me alone. I am fed up of you."

Aina shouted, "I will not leave you alone to enjoy yourself. I will stay with you right here."

"Why should I listen to you?" asked Daman.

"Because of the secret of your birth, you will do as I say. Is that clear?" asked Aina firmly.

Daman shouted, "Yes. Yes, damn you. I hate you."

Aina said, "I don't have the inclination nor the time to hate you. I don't think you are so important that I should expend my energy to hate you! You are nothing for me but a pain. I am just indifferent to you."

Daman felt insulted. Aina went to her bedroom and lay down on her bed. She heard Daman going out.

Aina thought, "I must find out more about Daman. I will search his study today."

She went to his study and carefully she started looking around. In one drawer she saw a receipt for a revolver. He had bought it a month back. Aina opened another drawer of the table. She froze. A shining new revolver was kept in it. She just shut the drawer without touching anything, with her mind buzzing with questions.

Why had he purchased a revolver? Was it for her? She jumped with shock as suddenly the doorbell rang. She ran to the door, after checking that Daman would not be able to make out that she had been to his study. Daman may have come back but why wasn't he using his key? Where were the servants? The doorbell rang again. She opened the door. Heera was standing there. She took him to her room. He sat on her bed and held her to him. Aina started pouring out her agonies.

"Heera. Daman is gay, just like you suspected all along," said Aina.

"This is good in a way. It may give you grounds for taking a divorce from him," said Heera.

She rested her head against his strong shoulder, because it was the only thing that was giving her security and asked, "You know how to make me feel better. You are so good. Don't move. I am feeling very comfortable."

Aina went on talking but when she told Heera about Daman keeping a revolver Heera became worried.

He said, "That can be dangerous. You should be very careful. Why don't you run away with me?"

Aina said "No Heera. Where will we run away? They will run after us. We have to face life head-on."

"Aina, we will find another way," said Heera.

"But there is no other way. Do you know Heera, you can file a suit for Daman's property."

"How is that possible Aina?"

"Girdhari told me that Daman is your father's son through my mother-in-law, Ram Katori."

Heera stood immobile for a long time. Aina became worried at his frozen face and silent reaction.

Then Heera said, "This explains why my father wanted me to stay on in this house."

"Would you like to put a claim to the property Heera?" asked Aina.

"No Aina. It would mar the name of my father. I would not like that at all. He was an extremely respected person. I don't want any property at the cost of the good reputation of my father," said Heera firmly.

The matter was closed and Aina never repeated it again, because she realized that this piece of news had actually hurt Heera. To change the subject and to lighten the atmosphere, Aina exclaimed, "Heera. I am so happy that we are together again. It has been so terrible without you. I felt lonely, depressed and afraid."

"My poor darling, you are too good to suffer at the hands of the likes of Daman. I will not let him harm you. Now you have no duty towards Daman. Marry me. I will never let you down. You can bank on me always. Whatever is mine, is yours. I love you, my dearest."

Aina said, "Heera. My life is incomplete without you. I love you. Life is worthwhile only because of you."

Then they discussed how to meet again and Heera went back to his house. Aina lay down in her own bedroom. She thought about her present situation.

It was clear that Daman did not want her. Now he wanted that Aina should go away. That would be the best solution for Daman, as for his elections he would be a married man yet without Aina troubling him. But the fact that she had caught him with Manav and had come to know their secret, might end up in their planning to remove her from Daman's life. They would be afraid that she would tell their secret to the world. Would they go to the extent of killing her so that their secret would remain safe? Is that why he had bought a revolver? A tremor of fear ran through her. She needed to be very careful.

CHAPTER 29

After that, as time passed, Aina tried to avoid being alone with Daman. She stayed in her room and through the maid servant, Daman came to know that Aina wasn't well. As time passed, one day Aina told Daman that she had started feeling very sick.

He just grunted, "Show yourself to the doctor."

After some days when she was sick again, he became angry, "Why don't you go to the doctor?"

She said, "I have shown the doctor. I am pregnant."

She thought, "I wonder what he is thinking because he has never made love to me till now."

His face was a treat to watch. First there was total surprise and shock, then disbelief and panic that settled into a deep hurt, and lastly a state of anger which made him hiss out the words, "You are a slut."

"And what are you Daman?" she asked sweetly as he glared at her and walked off in a huff.

Daman stayed in his study that day. He did not go anywhere except to call his mother to tell her the news. Before sleeping, Aina heard Daman again talking to his mother on the telephone. Aina revelled in it. She could sense his frustration, but finally they won again.

He told his mother that on second thoughts, he was feeling very triumphant about the situation as Aina's pregnancy would prove to the world that he was a man, what if he himself knew that the child was not his!

Now the rumour about him would stop as people would believe that he was normal and virile.

Aina thought, "Daman is so strange. He did not even ask who the father of the child is. Only I know the wonderful fact that this is Heera's child and that is why the child is so precious to me." Aina was really happy.

From that day onwards, Daman enjoyed telling other people that Aina was pregnant. He seemed proud of the fact, though in his heart, he must have felt wretched, as he knew that their marriage was never consummated. For her part Aina felt that she had got a new lease of life because now Daman would want her alive.

Aina met Heera and told him the happy news. He was delighted with the news that he was to become a father. As time passed, they met off and on whenever possible. Heera would put his hand on her stomach and would love to feel the child inside. Aina lost her fear that Daman would harm her and she enjoyed her pregnancy, more so because whenever they met, she could see the thrill on the face of Heera as he felt the baby inside.

Aina had never been so happy. She never felt guilty or ashamed about Heera or the child. Rather she felt blessed that she was carrying her beloved Heera's child in her womb. She was in high spirits. There was a beautiful glow on her face. Ram Katori came to meet her once, but that could not puncture Aina's happiness as Ram Katori was careful with Aina and kept her distance.

So life proceeded in a happy manner where Aina forced herself not to think of her problems. She just concentrated on being happy so that her dearest baby and Heera too would be happy. Time rolled on and

Aina also waddled. But still Daman stayed away from Aina.

Aina was surprised one day when Ram Katori again came to their new house. Aina was in her own room when she heard Ram Katori say to Daman, "I am thinking of throwing a party for the child. You must now celebrate it with style. Decorate and illuminate every part of the house in such a way that it glows in the night."

Daman said, "No, we cannot illuminate our house from outside, because our country has just started fighting a war. Every citizen has to put black paper on the windows and ventilators, so that no light can be seen by any enemy plane that may come to attack us. We in Rojpur have to be more careful, because the airfield is near our town. So we cannot put lights outside."

Ram Katori was loathe to give up. She said, "Then decorate and illuminate the interiors so much that the hall looks like a fairyland. Spare no expense. Let our party be the talk of the town. And you must call your wife's family. They should see what a grand lifestyle we have. And I also want to see what they bring for the child. I am sure the paupers will have nothing to give."

So Ram Katori called her relatives over in the ninth month of Aina's pregnancy for the 'Gode Bharai' (baby shower) ceremony in which they kept a doll, fruits, dry fruits and sweets in her lap and blessed her to have a healthy child. On the day of the celebration, Ram Katori acted as the perfect mother-in-law and Aina seemed to be an ideal daughter-in-law for the benefit of the guests. In the evening Aina got ready for the party eagerly.

She was excited because she knew that her parents would be coming. She desperately wanted to see her parents. They still meant so much to her. She stood in the hall. It was decorated beautifully.

Then Aina looked around and thought, "Daman has spared no expense in putting up a grand show to tell the world that he is to become a father. Today he will prove to the whole world that he is a virile man."

Numerous guests started coming and they were congratulating Daman for his child.

And the devil came into her. She thought, "Should I tell the world that the child is not his? Daman knows the facts and despite his seeming joy, I can see him feeling bad about it. Oh! How I love that!"

Aina acted on this impulse and instantly she walked to Daman and said, "Come at once to my room. I have to talk to you. It is very important."

Surprisingly Daman followed her immediately.

When Daman entered her room, she said, "I want a divorce."

Daman spoke fiercely but in a hushed tone, "Are you off your head? I can't give you a divorce. It will harm my chances of getting a party ticket because divorce has a stigma attached to it. You can go to your house with your family today, but I will not give you a divorce."

"I will not go till you give me a divorce. If you don't, I will tell the world that this child is not yours."

Daman flared up, "No, you will not tell anything to anyone."

"Daman, give me in writing that you will give me a divorce and a good alimony or I will tell everyone."

"Aren't you ashamed of behaving in this manner?" snarled Daman.

"Aren't you ashamed of marrying me when you were gay?" questioned Aina.

"There are so many guests outside. I have to go," Daman started walking outside.

"There are so many guests outside, so more people will hear that you are gay and you have not sired this child. Go Daman. But if you don't want the people to know the truth, then give me in writing."

Totally cornered, Daman moved towards Aina aggressively, but Aina said calmly, "If you come one step ahead, I will shoot you." And she pointed a revolver at Daman. It was Daman's own revolver.

Daman blanched. He sat down then and wrote out on her writing pad that he agreed to give a divorce to Aina and he would also give a good alimony. He thrust the paper in Aina's hand and grunted, "If you dare say anything outside, I will kill you." Daman walked off and Aina flopped on her bed completely drained.

After some time she felt strong enough to join the party. She felt that she had achieved something, but she knew that she had increased the risk to her life. Her one security was that Daman would do nothing till she was pregnant. He could not be so ruthless as to hurt the baby in her womb, specially when it proved his potency.

She saw her family arrive and she walked ahead to meet them. She sighted Sabal chacha and welcomed him. Then she saw her mother. She smiled with genuine love and walked towards her and then she saw another person getting down. Her brother Munna and then another, his wife, Sonali.

And now Aina's face froze. Sonali was wearing the necklace that Aina had given her mother to pay off the debts. It was the same distinctive necklace that Ram

Katori had given to Aina on her wedding day. She looked around and saw her angry mother-in-law Ram Katori and realized that she too was staring at Sonali's necklace.

Ram Katori turned and looked at Aina and then yelled, "You liar! You thief! You take our jewellery and pass it on to your relatives and then tell us lies that they were stolen! How despicable of you!"

Aina felt life ebbing from her. She braced herself for more trouble as she saw Daman coming on the scene. But he surprised her by telling his mother, "Quiet. Don't make a scene here, Mataji. Later."

Everyone walked off leaving Aina with her family. There was no tear, not even one in Aina's eyes. She knew what 'later' meant. She would be given a fitting punishment, but she would face that later. She went to her family saying, "You all are not welcome here. Let us go out of the gate. Where is Papa?"

"He hasn't come as he is not well," said Gomti.

Aina said, "Sabal chacha. You go inside and have dinner. I want to talk to my family."

Sabal went away inside and Aina then said, "Well all of you. Thank you for coming and now this is the last time you all are showing your faces to me. Ma you have betrayed me. I gave the jewellery so that you could pay your debts, but you gave them to Sonali."

"Aina she had nothing nice to wear. I had to keep up our and your prestige," said her mother.

"And she had to wear this very necklace of my mother-in-law, which is so distinctive, right to my in-law's house? Moreover I told you not to forgive Munna and his wife, but you have seemingly not only forgiven them, but also accepted them back in your family."

Ma said, "Munna has lost his job in his in-law's business. His father-in-law died and his brothers-in-law turned him out. So Sonali and Munna have come back to us. Sonali is a changed person now. Munna has also apologized to us very sincerely for all that he did."

Aina said, "Because he has no money and at your place he can manage on the money I send every month. The fact is that I have had enough of you all. I am not connected with you all from today. I won't send any money either. The bond has snapped mother, because of your betrayal. I felt for you and you have let me down. A son is always dear. The daughter may die in her efforts but it is the son who gets full preference. Now no more. I am washing my hands off you all. I am totally free from the promise I made to you. I have suffered so much, just because I did not want you upset. But now I will live life as I want. I always thought how you could send me back to this hell. You always made me do what you wanted and that also by making me swear on you. It was just because you did not want your life and Munna's life upset with a married daughter coming back to stay in your house. You are as selfish as the others. Don't expect anything from me anymore. You are not worth my love. I am free of you all forever. Thank you, now go."

CHAPTER 30

They went and no one stopped them. Aina stood there like a statue. Her eyes burned for a moment, but just a moment. Then she thought, 'I am brave. I depend on myself only. I smile always. Just celebrate life,' and her eyes crinkled into a smile as she yelled in her thoughts, "This is my day of deliverance from all the bonds that God tied me to, when he sent me to this family. I am truly free now and from today I am going to enjoy my freedom. I am glad even Heera is not here. No, that is a lie. This house feels so empty without Heera. Why didn't he come tonight? I wish he was here."

Suddenly she heard her mother's voice saying, "Aina. Sonali gave me this necklace to return to you. See how great she is. She could have kept the necklace. The rest of the jewellery you gave, we sold that to pay off all the debts, otherwise I would have returned everything to you. I have to say that you should forget whatever has happened. Keep this necklace and don't break relations with us otherwise you will remain totally alone."

"Why shouldn't I, Ma? You have always loved Munna, not me. I loved you so much but you never loved me. You have not been a good mother to me."

Gomti's face stiffened for a moment and then she said, "That is because I am not your real mother," and she started walking away. It took a few moments for Aina to understand the import of what her mother had said. Then Aina ran towards Gomti and she caught her arm and asked, "What did you say just now?"

"I said that I am not your mother and that is the truth. Now leave me," said Gomti.

"I will not leave you till you tell me in detail. You have shaken my very existence, how can you go away as if nothing has happened?" shouted Aina.

"Don't shout. I haven't told this to anyone, not even to Munna. At my mother's house, when I gave birth to an eunuch, I couldn't accept him. Your father came to see me. I told him that I could not keep the eunuch child and I would not go home without a child or everyone would taunt me again. Then your father brought you to me and put you in my lap and said that you were the only newborn available. You became my daughter. I told everyone in the house that you were born to me."

"How many other people know who I am?" asked Aina.

"No one, only your father and I know. My parents knew but both are dead," said Gomti.

"And what about Munna?" asked Aina.

"Munna is my own son," said Gomti and she did not know how wounded Aina felt.

Gomti said, "Forget everything. You have no one in the world. Don't cut your ties with our family."

"Thank you Gomtiji for adopting me and looking after me. It was very kind of you," said Aina.

"Shut up Aina. Don't talk like this," said Gomti.

"Who was my mother? Did anyone come later to claim me?" asked Aina.

Gomti said, "No one came to claim you. Only your father knows who you are."

Then Gomti kept the necklace in Aina's hand and walked off saying, "Munna is waiting for me. Now I better hurry." And she had gone away leaving so many questions in Aina's benumbed brain. The party was already going on well and Aina walked inside the house.

She was walking without realizing what was happening around her. All that she was aware was a searing pain in her heart and a deep ache in her stomach where the child was moving. But all that she could think of was a wasted life that she had endured to appease a mother who had always been indifferent to her and was not her mother at all. And now Daman would be mad at her. There was no knowing what he would do. He was capable of anything.

Aina knew that Sabal chacha could protect her from Daman's wrath. She tried to find Sabal, but she could not see him anywhere. She found it difficult to stand, so she left the party. She went to her room and she felt like howling and screaming to ease the pain in her heart, but she steeled her will and did not allow even a groan to come out. She thought, "I am totally free, without any bondage. I can live independently. I will survive, come what may. I have a very strong will power. I can weather any storm that comes my way."

She sat down on the bed and breathed deeply. Now she had to think about what her husband would do when the party finished. He would certainly scold her for what had happened. Would he kill her? She trembled.

Daman came to her later when the party had finished and only a few relatives were left in the house. He came with a deliberate air and kicked her. She had not prepared herself for this. She was quick to evade his foot. But the quick movement gave her a sharp pain. She had not dreamt that he would want to harm her when she was pregnant with a child. She was proud of herself. Despite the shock and agony, she did not shed a single tear. She said calmly, "So you hit me because you have shown the world that you are a man. Now you don't need a child to prove anything to anyone."

Daman sneered, "Why throw blame on me when you are tainted? What have you done? You told me a lie that the jewellery was stolen in the train. You gave it to your family. Doesn't that amount to stealing and lying?"

Aina shouted, "And what about you? You have been so nasty and heartless towards me. You married me though you were gay. You spoilt my life."

He kicked again but she was fully prepared this time and when he was least expecting it, she got up with a superhuman effort and ran. He stopped her.

"Who is the father of your child?" he rasped. His hands on her arm were brutal. They left red weals.

She shouted, "It is none of your business."

He raised his hand to hit her and then she retaliated. She hit him between his legs. Then as quickly as she could, she ran outside into the hall where all the relatives were still sitting.

She shouted, "Save me. Daman is kicking my stomach to kill my baby."

She saw Daman come limping behind her after a few minutes. She saw him realize that she had told the relatives. She felt him stop behind her. He had not been expecting her to make this public declaration. Her mother-in-law was certainly a quick thinker.

She shouted, "Folks what do you expect when my son suspects that the child is not his."

Daman shouted, "What are you saying Mataji? Shut up. The child is mine."

His mother went pale and said meekly, "Of course it is."

For once she had made a gaffe and had not realized that what she had said went against her own son. Aina saw Sabal, then she stammered, "Daman was trying to kill my unborn child. Oooooh! It is paining so badly. I think he has already killed my baby. Sabal chacha. Take me to the hospital at once."

Aina screamed with pain. Sabal took her to the hospital and stayed with her. She refused to meet anyone else. She just had Sabal tell them that she had lost her baby. She did not shed a single tear.

She did not allow her family to come and meet her. She refused to let her mother come in, even though she stood outside and begged her to. Ram Katori too seemed really upset at losing her little grandchild. Aina would not speak to her either. In the hospital room, Aina would just meet Sabal chacha and talk to him.

The next day her brother Laila came to the hospital saying, "Oh! God bless the little baby."

Her mother-in-law shouted, "Why is an eunuch coming in when there has been a tragedy?"

By this time, Laila had already come into Aina's room. He said, "Has there been a tragedy here? Oh! I was misinformed. I am sorry, sister. I am going now. Everything will be all right. Take care of yourself."

Aina folded her hands and said, "Thank you, brother."

No one was the wiser, Aina hoped, but if they were, then she did not care any more because she had nothing more to lose, so where was the fear? She had now choked the neck of every fear and now she was really and truly free. No more panic. She would be in control always. And in her mind she imagined herself telling Daman point blank, "I am so happy to be free of you. Now I am going to celebrate life."

But where was Heera? Aina was really worried. Then he came to see her. On the day of the party he had met with an accident and he had been injured. Now he had recovered enough to be able to meet Aina.

CHAPTER 31

She allowed another person to come. Her father. She asked Sabal to call him. Kalka had become weak and he walked in nervously, asking, "How are you Aina?"

"I am better Papa. The pain is less now," said Aina.

"Aina, I again ask you to forgive me for marrying you into such a family. I was the one who had seen Daman before your marriage. I should have put my foot down before you were married there."

Aina said, "Yes Papa. I have suffered and I will forgive you only if you do something for me. I want to know who my parents are. Who is my mother? Who is my father? I want to meet them."

Kalka said, "I don't know how you will take it. Well the facts are that when I was called by Gomti after the birth of Laila, I reached a day late as another child had been born and that was you."

"To whom Papa, who is my mother?" asked Aina.

"Don't ask Aina. Let the past be. Let it remain dead. You will hurt to know the truth," said Kalka.

"I am no longer weak Papa. I am strong. I can hear anything. Tell me honestly," said Aina.

Kalka said with a resigned expression, "When Gomti did not want to keep that child, yet would not return to our house without a child, I was worried. Then an angel in disguise gave her child to me."

"Who was that angel?" asked Aina impatiently.

"I will get her. She is sitting outside," said Kalka.

Aina saw her father walk outside and then she felt a curious mixture of fear and excitement. She saw Kalka leading in an old woman who looked nervous.

Aina looked at her face and thought, "I have seen her somewhere." She couldn't recollect at first and the woman came towards Aina.

Then Aina gasped, "Bijli! You are my mother!"

"Oh! I am sorry Aina. I know it will disappoint you to learn that I am your mother, but I couldn't see your father so worried. That night when he came and told me that his wife was suffering trauma, I knew I had to give you to her. Forgive me Aina, my baby," said Bijli.

"Why did you give me away?" asked Aina.

"I knew how worried your father was. I could also understand the pain of Gomti. But worse was the fact that I knew that you had no future with me. I did not want to make you a prostitute".

"So you became very selfless and gave the darling daughter whom you loved more than life itself, to the person you loved the most. It must have cut you up."

"It did, Aina. I was near demented after I had given you."

"Who is my father?" asked Aina nervously.

"Your father Kalka is your real father. I loved him from the beginning and I was always true to him. The only thing missing in our relationship was the ritual of a marriage," said Bijli.

"Do you love me?" asked Aina.

"More than myself. More than everyone. I love you my angel, my darling child," said Bijli. Aina threw her arms around Bijli and she wept. Bijli and Aina both cried, clutching each other as if afraid to let go.

Then Bijli drew away and asked, "Does it hurt you that I was a prostitute when I was young?"

"No. Moreover you were not a prostitute. You were just a dancing girl. You were true to my father and you made him happy and you love me. Nothing else matters to me, Ma," said Aina.

"I have been yearning to hear you call me Ma. It is like a balm to my soul. Oh bless you my darling daughter! I love you so much. I have craved to hold you in my arms," said Bijli lovingly.

"Ma, how could you live without me all these years?" asked Aina.

"I couldn't. It was torture and so I begged your father to take me to his house so that I could see my darling daughter grow up. And he is such a wonderful person, that despite everything he took me to see you. Remember? I met you. You have a wonderful father."

"Now I have a wonderful mother too. I am so lucky that you are my mother. I remember that first meeting with you. I thought you were a fairy. I am sorry I was rude to you. It must have hurt you. Now I want to make up for that. I won't let you leave me ever. You have to stay with me," said Aina.

"What are you saying? How can I live with you? Everyone knows that I was a prostitute," said Bijli.

"But I want the world to know my loving mother."

"No Aina, my child. I don't want to hurt your father in any way and this will reflect on him and his family. It is enough to be able to see him and you sometimes. These will be blessings enough."

Kalka said, "If you want our help with Daman let us know. Sabal will deal with him."

"Yes Papa. I will let you know if I need help but just now tell me something. How many people knew that I am Bijli's, I mean Ma's daughter?" asked Aina.

"No one else knew except Prasad Chacha and Girish whom I met at the railway station, when I had you in my arms. For the rest, we have kept the secret and not told anyone about it," said Kalka.

Aina thought, "That explains why Girish chose to torment me to spite Mahavir Baba."

"Now Aina you must rest," said Bijli.

"Only if you promise to meet me everyday," said Aina holding her hand.

"Yes I promise," said Bijli.

And Heera, who was also there, took them to his house. Bijli kept her promise and came to meet Aina everyday. Aina felt very happy because she realized what a wonderful, loving, caring and kind person her mother was. Just what she wanted a mother to be! For the first time in her life, unheld by any thread, slave to no relationship, she felt totally free because her real mother and father accepted her for what she was. Her mother Bijli's love was unconditional and constant, inspite of everything. Aina had found the love she craved for.

Gomti had never given her this feeling of security. Yet in Aina there was no feeling of vengeance to make Gomti learn a lesson. She wanted to live for her mother Bijli and for her new found relationships and love. On Bijli's insistence, they decided that they would not tell Gomti the real fact about Bijli being the real mother, because it would hurt her smug world which comprised of only Munna and Sonali. Bijli decided that they would not disturb Gomti's haven of contentment.

Aina thought how great her mother Bijli was. She was giving as well as forgiving, even at the cost of so much suffering. But Aina did not feel the same emotions. She did not feel like forgiving Daman. She would not let Daman free. She would stick to her demands and see him squirm.

On being discharged from the hospital, Heera felt that Aina should not return to Daman's house as there was danger to her life, but Aina insisted that she needed to go there first.

She said, "I have to go there. I promise you that I will come back to your house soon."

Heera exclaimed, "Aina I will die if something happens to you."

Aina said, "Don't worry, I will be very careful. Let me do this Heera. I have been a spineless creeper too long. I have been depending on others all the time. Let me be self sufficient now."

Heera said, "I am afraid for you Aina. You are pitted against two. Both Daman and Manav are without compunction for anyone. If I can be of any use, let me know. I want to help you."

But Aina insisted and she returned to her husband's new house. So when Daman came home, he saw her sitting coyly on the sofa. She could see that Daman was shocked on seeing her.

Daman said, "Why have you come? Go away."

Aina replied, "This is my house too. I will not leave it. You can't force me to go away."

"Go to your room then. I don't want to see your face. Get lost." But she didn't obey him.

Aina knew that now they were like two enemies in the same house. Daman straightaway went out of the house and Aina was left alone. She revelled in her solitude now and enjoyed the fact that now she could do what she wanted. She used the time to sift through some files in Daman's study, but she could not find anything incriminating. Suddenly she heard the front door open.

CHAPTER 32

Aina felt petrified. Quickly she hid behind the floor length curtain. Daman came into the study quickly. Thankfully he was alone. He had his back to her. She peeped out to see. He opened a drawer with a key and Aina saw a revolver kept in it. Either he had bought a new one or maybe in her absence he had checked her room and found his revolver that she had taken.

Then with his key he opened another lock and Aina was surprised. The key opened a secret flat panel. There were papers in that. Daman kept another file in it and started closing it. Suddenly Daman started sniffing. He muttered, "What is this perfume? Aina puts on this perfume. Has she come into my study? I must check."

Aina felt terrified as Daman got up to investigate. Aina felt that she would be caught and then Daman would not spare her. He started looking around and he had come just near the curtain she was hiding behind, when the doorbell rang and a servant came and told Daman that some people had come to meet him. Daman told the servant, "Take them to the drawing room."

Daman then closed the secret panel and kept the key in a drawer. Aina saw Daman walk out and she bided her time, then quickly she ran from the study to her room. She looked around for the revolver that she had put in her room, and couldn't find it. She thought, "So Daman must have searched my room and taken it."

The next day she got ready. She had finished her breakfast, when Aina heard someone shouting. She went to see what had happened because she had recognized the voices of her mother-in-law and Daman. Ram Katori had come to visit them.

Aina hid behind a pillar and listened. Ram Katori was saying, "You have to stay married to Aina, Daman. It is an order. You must keep up the pretense."

Daman retorted, "You want me married and that woman wants a divorce. I am feeling squashed between the two of you. I have blindly obeyed you till now, but now I am going to do what I want. Don't bully me."

"What about your secret, Daman?"

"Mataji. You also have your secret that I am not my father's son. Do you think this doesn't hurt me? I will not be dictated by anyone any more. I will decide about everything in my life now, of my own free will."

Daman had walked out of her room and now he rushed towards the staircase. He was really angry.

Ram Katori ran after him and said, "What will society say? Aina does not hinder your style of living. You live your life. Let it continue like this, Daman at least till I die. After that you can do what you want to do."

"Is your death all that I have to wait for complete deliverance? Then why wait for death?" shouted Daman angrily and he pushed Ram Katori. She was too near the steps. She tripped, lost her balance and she fell down the stairs. She fell in a crumpled heap and then Daman seemed to realize what he had done to his own mother.

He rushed down and then like a madman he shouted for the servants. Ram Katori was taken to the hospital after the servants had been sworn to secrecy not to disclose to anyone that she had been pushed down, but Aina knew that she had got another ace to play whenever Daman was nasty towards her.

Daman had perforce to stay with Ram Katori in the hospital and Aina got her chance. Aina made the most of this opportunity to get evidence against Daman. Aina took the papers of the bank account in her name. She also took the paper in which Daman had written that he would be ready to give a divorce and alimony to her.

Then she went to Daman's study. She knew that Daman did not trust anyone. Manav was his gay partner. He would certainly have some guarantee from Manav so that he could trust Manav always. So she opened the drawer in which she had seen Daman keeping the key to the secret panel. She found the key and she opened the secret compartment. It contained personal information that Daman would not want the world to know.

She found the receipts that Manav had given for the money he had taken from Daman. She took that file. She found a paper Manav had signed that he would never leave Daman. She found papers about illegal transactions amounting to smuggling that certainly could incriminate Daman in the eyes of the law.

Aina thought, "It had been ever so scary when I had been hiding behind the curtain yesterday, but this is well worth the scare." Now she made sure that Daman's study looked the same and then she went to her room. Aina quickly kept everything in her suitcase and she was about to leave the house, when she thought that she would carry some more books from the library.

Aina rushed to the library room in the house. She quickly picked up three novels and she was about to return when she heard a strange squeaky voice nearby. Suddenly cautious, she slowly moved towards the sound which was coming from the room at the far end of the corridor. Heera had told Aina that this room had been given to Rocoo to stay in, when Aina had been in the hospital. She tiptoed closer towards the sound.

Suddenly she heard a voice speak something which was not coherent to her. She edged closer to the sound and then she was just near the door connected to the corridor outside the library. She stepped into the long corridor and went to the door of his room. She heard the squeaky sound again. It was the sound of a trans-receiver.

She then heard Rocoo's voice speak, "Till now everything is going according to our plan. Daman Rai is not suspicious of me at all. So now my plan is that on this 8th, Monday night, Tuesday morning, by 0130 hours, I will put five lights on the top of his house which is 10 miles north of the Defence airfield. Give me 30 minutes to escape. Attack at 0200 hours. Over." Again the voice squeaked and Rocoo said, "OK. Over and out."

Tall vase stands stood along the corridor. Aina moved to run away and a vase stand fell. Aina nearly screamed at the unexpected sound. But then she heard the sound of a chair scraping and quick footsteps. Aina's heart started beating rapidly. Afraid that now Rocoo could catch her, she moved quickly away from the door and ran stealthily into the library. She hid behind the curtain of the window which opened into the corridor.

She jumped with fright as she heard Rocoo shouting quite near her, "Who is it?" If Rocoo had just extended his arm, he could have touched her. She dared not move. Aina froze and tried to quieten her breathing as Rocoo walked around checking the library. Soon Rocoo was coming closer towards her hiding place.

Aina moved fast. She sat on the window sill and leaned over. She pushed another vase-stand down. It fell with a clatter. Rocoo ran out to check and then thankfully Rocoo went down the corridor and Aina got her chance. She ran across the library.

It took a lot of dodging for her to reach her room safely without being seen by Rocoo. After she reached her room, she lay down for some minutes trying to get her breath back. Later she picked up her suitcase and bag. She paused for a while to listen carefully for any movement outside. Then she ran out of her room.

She stopped to check the corridor which ended in Rocoo's room. She saw Rocoo walking back towards his room. She kept on waiting till Rocoo had reached his room. He looked back once and she ducked back behind a pillar. When he had shut the door of his room, she ran out of the house as fast as she could. She quickly took a rickshaw and went to Heera's house, all the time looking back to verify that Rocoo was not coming after her.

CHAPTER 33

Heera was still working for Daman and Ram Katori, more because he wanted to know what was transpiring in their house. He saw that Ram Katori had survived but she was paralysed for life and that Daman had employed a maid servant to look after Ram Katori in the old house. He felt pity for Ram Katori who couldn't even speak. Tears rolled down her cheeks as she sat helplessly in her wheelchair.

Heera felt really very sorry for her when the unscrupulous Daman came the next day to their old house where Ram Katori still lived alone. Daman just caught his mother's hand roughly and forced her thumb impressions on the legal papers that transferred all her property and wealth to Daman.

Suddenly Daman turned towards Heera and said, "Do you know where Aina is?"

Heera answered, "Why are you asking me? You should know where your wife is."

Daman exclaimed, "Don't act innocent, Heera. I do know where she is. She is at your house. Why have you given shelter to Aina? You work for us and so your loyalty should be towards us."

Heera replied, "I have to answer to God also and I can't support you when you are in the wrong, and now you are doing wrong things as a habit. Stop being evil or you will end up in jail."

Daman suddenly felt a rage sweep over him and he spoke angrily, "How dare you criticise me! From today you are dismissed from your job here. Don't show your face from tomorrow."

Daman gave the money due to Heera and he took all the keys from Heera, and then he said, "I should not see you in my house anymore. Get lost."

Heera grinned and said, "Oh Daman! How rude you have become, you naughty boy! This is not how you should speak to your brother; specially a brother who can claim your whole property. So learn some manners, you moron."

"You my brother? Claim on property? What do you mean?" snarled Daman.

"Go and ask your mother. I might just file a suit for your inheritance," answered Heera and he walked out of the house cheerfully, leaving Daman seething in a state of confusion, embarassment, fear and incredulity.

Heera returned home and told everyone, "I have got freedom from my employers. Daman has chucked me out from my job. Don't worry. I have already got another job where I have to join after a month, so it suits me fine. I am well rid of that dreadful Daman."

Sabal, Bijli, Kalka and Laila congratulated Heera for the new job, then they started talking about Aina.

Heera said, "I think then Aina should file a suit for divorce."

Sabal answered, "If Aina asks for a divorce, she won't get alimony."

Heera replied, "I don't care if Aina does not get alimony. I don't want Daman's money."

Then Heera turned to Kalka and Bijli and said, "I love your daughter and I want to marry her as soon as possible. I promise I will look after her. I have substantial money of my own. Now I have a job and I am sure that we will be able to manage quite comfortably. I will wait for Aina to be free even if it takes a lifetime. I want your permission to marry Aina when she gets her divorce."

Kalka looked at Bijli and she nodded.

Kalka said, "I will be very happy to see Aina marry you. We give our permission to you. But what I am afraid of, is that Daman may try to harm Aina."

Bijli agreed, "What I am also concerned about is the danger to Aina's life whether the divorce goes through or not, because Daman will always be afraid that she will tell his secrets to the world. We should first do something about her security, because Daman seems to be an extremely vindictive person."

Just then Aina came running in. Seeing her so distraught, they made her sit down before she could tell them what the matter was. Then Aina related what she had heard and then she said, "I think something very grave is happening. I think Rocoo is a spy. Rojpur is so near the Defence airfield. We should be careful."

Bijli asked, "I don't understand this."

Aina said, "Because a war is going on, we are following black outs here in Rojpur and the other places near the Defence airfield. Rocoo will put lights on the terrace so that it is easy for enemy planes to bombard the airfield. Then he seems to be planning to escape."

Heera said, "I think this is a very serious matter. He is a traitor towards our country, but we need to keep up pretences that we don't know about all this. Ofcourse we should let the Air Force police know about this grave threat. Whatever happens, we should be careful. Rocoo seems to be a dangerous man."

Aina said, "We all will have to take precautions. Ma and Laila should go away from here because if Daman comes here, probably Rocoo will come also. He may resort to violence."

Bijlee argued, "We will not go anywhere. We will see this through. You should go, Aina. The danger is to you. You never know how Daman will react to your demand for a divorce. What should we do about it?"

Aina said, "I think we should not file a divorce suit yet. Only threatening him with a divorce suit will have more effect on him. It will leave more scope for negotiations. If we file a suit straightaway, he would just try to kill me and use Rocoo for this."

"Don't talk like that Aina," gasped Bijli.

"Ma, Daman is a very ruthless man. He carries grudges too. He will not let me out easily. And if they come here, please don't let on that we know that Rocoo is a spy, till it is absolutely necessary."

Laila called from inside, "Ma, please come here."

Bijlee went inside. Suddenly there was some commotion outside and the door was forced open by a belligerent Daman with Manav and Rocoo. They barged into the house unannounced. Kalka, Sabal, Aina and Heera were sitting in the living room.

Heera said politely, "Oh! Welcome. Please sit down."

Manav snarled, "Shut up! You traitor. What is the reason that you are taking her side?"

Heera said, "Because she is in the right. Daman is in the wrong. He has spoilt her life because of you Manav. It is pitiable that Daman does not know what a fraud you are Manav. You just want his money."

Manav became red with anger and he yelled, "You are the fraud. I bet you cheated in his accounts."

Heera smiled and said in an even voice, "Don't think that everyone thinks and acts like you three do."

Aina spoke up, "Daman have you come here to tell me that you are ready to give me a divorce?"

Daman said, "I will not give you a divorce and that is it. Now do what you want to do."

Aina said, "That is fine by me. I will file a suit in court."

"You will do nothing of the kind," replied Daman and he pulled out a revolver and put it on Aina's temple.

Aina said, "You cannot kill me because you are ambitious. You want to stand for an election. If you become a murderer, then you will not get a party ticket. If you don't give me a divorce, I will tell everyone; but if you give me a divorce, I will not reveal your secrets."

"But I want to finish your chapter for ever. So it is better that I kill you and your body is not found by the police," retorted Daman in a menacing and nasty voice, as he put his finger on the trigger, ready to shoot.

Heera said calmly, "Daman, this house is in the middle of a busy market place. If you shoot her here, everyone outside will come to know."

"Haven't you heard of a silencer? No one will hear the guns and you all will be dead," said Rocoo.

Heera said, "But think logically. How will you three escape from here? People will see you. If you leave our dead bodies here, people will tell the police that they saw you three enter. The people around my house like me a lot because I am not evil like you all."

Rocoo said, "Shut up, Heera. Don't try these tricks with us. And why are you worrying about us? Worry about yourselves. It is pack-up time for you all now. Make your last wish Heera."

Heera laughed loudly and replied, "My last wish is that you should throw each other into the same well."

"Shut up. It is not a joking matter," snarled Manav.

Daman said, "Come to think of it, Heera is right. Killing Aina would be enough and that we can do outside too. Come on, Manav and Rocoo, let us go."

Daman started pulling Aina towards the front door.

CHAPTER 34

Heera said, "Do you think we will keep quiet when you take Aina away? You are such a fool Daman."

Manav shouted, "Stop it you idiot. Just shut up. Now just remember your God, because it is the end for all of you. I have had enough of this nonsense. Daman do as I say. Just kill her and be done with it."

Daman pointed his gun at Aina and just then Bijlee came into the room. She screamed and leapt to hold the hand of Daman, "Leave Aina. Take my life, but leave her. Don't kill her. She is too precious for all of us."

Trying to disentangle his arm from Bijlee, Daman said, "Go away. Aina knows my secrets. She has to die. Nobody can prevent that. So stop the theatrics."

Aina spoke up calmly, "Just a second, Daman. I will come with you of my own accord, but before that let me tell Rocoo and Manav about the secret panel."

Daman's hand slackened as he stared at Aina in bewilderment, and said, "No Aina. Keep quiet."

"But telling them won't hurt you because the panel in the study is empty," commented Aina.

"You dratted woman! Where are the papers? Give them to me," said Daman angrily.

Aina answered, "We have given all those papers to a lawyer who will get them published in a newspaper if anything happens to us. So kill me, but when that lawyer does not find me here, he will go straight to a news editor whom he knows, and he will get all the papers published, including the details of all your illegal actions like smuggling, that you have done. Then your truth will come out in front of the people. I wonder then if you will get a ticket for the elections. Now I am ready to die."

Rocoo said, "Yes, you have to die. Daman, don't care about what she is saying. None of the newspapers will print anything against you, Daman without showing the news to us. So let us take her out and kill her."

Rocoo pulled Aina and started dragging her towards the door. Heera pounced on Rocoo and there was a scuffle. Kalka then caught Daman. Sabal hit out at Manav. Heera caught Rocoo and took away his gun. Manav started hitting Heera. Even while holding Rocoo, Heera hit Manav so hard that he doubled up with pain.

Daman pushed Kalka away and pointed his revolver at Aina, saying, "Stop the fight. Don't move. Aina come outside or I will kill your father and uncle."

Aina said, "Daman, wait. I will come outside but for your good, I want to talk to you in private. If you don't talk to me now, you will regret it throughout your life."

Daman looked at her. Something in her serious face made him nod his head. Aina walked into the room nearby. They sat down and she told him all about what Rocoo had been speaking in his room on the trans-receiver.

She then said, "You must believe me. If Rocoo is caught, you will also be labelled a traitor as he works for you. I think you have sense enough that this is a very serious matter. I think you need to be very careful."

Daman paused and started thinking, although he felt cornered, but he realized he must cross check this.

Suddenly Daman said, "Aina, I shouldn't believe you, but I don't know why, I do believe you. This is really a serious matter. I don't want to confront Rocoo just now, because we have no evidence against him. I want him caught red handed. But I have my connections and I am going to call them first to check on Rocoo."

Daman used the telephone and called someone. He related the conversation that Aina had heard. Then he listened to the voice at the other end for some time.

When the call finished, Daman was really shaken. He was silent for a minute and then he said, "Aina you were right. The Defence authorities were already suspicious of Rocoo. Now, they will catch him red handed, but we should not tell anything to Rocoo."

Daman then walked to the outer room and said, "Manav and Rocoo. I have to give in to these people or my political career will be finished. You both go and talk to the chief about my candidature. I will have a final settlement with these people and then I will join you."

Manav and Rocoo seemed hesitant, but soon they walked away. Then everyone sat down and Daman said, "Aina. I must thank you for saving me from being labelled a traitor along with Rocoo. It would have ended my political career. Now, what do you want from me?"

Aina said, "I want a divorce from you."

Daman said in a subdued voice, "It will give me bad publicity that I can ill afford at this time."

Sabal suggested, "There is a way out in which both Aina and you will not get harmed. We can work out a divorce by mutual consent between you two. It will take time but I can try to get it done without undue publicity as I know the judges. And you know the newspaper people here. In this way the divorce will not hinder your political ambitions and you both can be free of each other."

Daman grunted his agreement to what Sabal proposed, and he walked out in a subdued manner.

The Air Force Commander Kumar called Daman to his office. They discussed the plan. Kumar came in plainclothes to the house and Daman made it a point to send Rocoo away. Kumar took a complete recka and then made a map. Kumar went to the terrace to make a personal assessment of how they could trap Rocoo. Daman promised all the co-operation they needed.

On the 8th, Monday night, Tuesday morning, everything seemed normal, but this normalcy was only superficial. Daman was alert regarding Rocoo and unobtrusively, he was keeping a watch on Rocoo.

On the face of it, Rocoo looked relaxed, but now Daman noticed that Rocoo was edgy. Daman also nonchalantly went about his usual routine work with Rocoo. Daman made it difficult for Rocoo by constantly making him work with him in his study. It was near about 10 in the night, that Rocoo complained of a headache.

Daman gave him some medicine and went on with their work. After half an hour, Rocoo fainted. Daman knew that he was feigning, but he acted as if Rocoo had really become unconscious. Daman spoke aloud, "Get up Rocoo. Oh! I must take Rocoo to the hospital."

In a minute Rocoo showed as if he had become conscious again. Then Daman let him go to his room.

While Rocoo had been in the study, Daman had left the front door open and a special posse of Air Force police headed by Commander Kumar had come in as planned. With alacrity they took up their positions. Some had gone to the terrace and taken their positions. Some went into the rooms from where they could keep an eye on Rocoo. Commander Kumar stayed on the terrace.

The security men who had hidden themselves in the library, which was closest to Rocoo's room, could hear Rocoo moving around. At 1 in the morning, Rocoo cautiously opened the door. The security men had been told that Rocoo should be caught redhanded only, when he was putting the lights on, to signal the enemy. So the security men remained hidden and moved noiselessly.

Stealthily Rocoo climbed the stairs with a bag on his back and a pistol and torch in his hands. He reached the terrace and bolted the door. It was a very dark night. The whole city was in darkness because of the black out. Rocoo looked around and satisfied that no one was around, he started laying down wires to put five lights.

By 1.20 he had finished the wiring for fixing the five lights. Now he had only to put in the plug in the socket. And then the security men converged on him. At first Rocoo was unaware about what was happening, but suddenly he sensed their presence. They first took his torch. All of a sudden he started shooting randomly all over the terrace. Downstairs Daman stiffened as he heard many shots being fired on the terrace, but he had very strict instructions not to come out. Finally the loud ear splitting booming of the shots stopped and all was silent. All this was done without lights so that if enemy planes came, they would not get a whiff of the location of the house and the Defence airfield nearby.

Four security men had caught Rocoo, but he was still struggling with them to reach the switchboard, as it was 1.30 and time for the five lights to be switched on. And the enemy plane came. Rocoo tried to free himself from the security men. He kicked and hit those around him and he used all his power to drag himself and the security men towards the switch. With a burst of energy he pulled the four people holding him towards the socket and stretched his hand to put in the plug.

But then Commander Kumar hit him on his jaw and tripped him over. Rocoo sprawled out on the floor. Quickly the other security men removed the plug, the wiring and the lights and they literally carried Rocoo through the terrace door to the stairs inside, even as anti aircraft guns started firing at the enemy plane. Then Air Force planes flew in to tackle the enemy plane. Kumar saw the dog fight of somersaults and attack between the enemy plane and their own planes. After a fierce tussle, the enemy plane flew back and the danger was over.

Daman could not stop himself. He came out of his room and stared at Rocoo being led away. Rocoo glared at him and shouted, "I will get you one day."

Then the security men took Rocoo away. It was all over the media that Rocoo was caught red handed. Daman became a hero for giving the authorities timely information about Rocoo being a dangerous spy.

Time rolled on after that and Heera and Aina had to show great patience. Subsequently, Sabal managed to get their divorce through, without publicity. As Daman had forced Ram Katori to give all the property to him, now as alimony, he gave one third of his wealth to Aina. Heera did not want the money, but Kalka insisted that they take the money. Kalka then put it in Aina's bank account as financial security for Aina and the baby. Yes, her baby Khushi (meaning happiness).

CHAPTER 35

Actually when Aina had been rushed to the hospital after Daman had kicked her, Aina had had a difficult labour, but her daughter had been born hale and hearty. From the hospital, Kalka, Bijli and Laila had taken the child, after they had explained the actual circumstances to the nice and helpful doctor. But the world had been told that the baby was no more.

Bijli, Laila, Heera and her baby Khushi had been living in Heera's house. This arrangement worked out very well for Aina, as her loved ones were near her.

Aina treasured her loved ones always, as she knew the true value of genuine love. Swami Ram who had prophesied unhappiness for her, had been proved wrong as her life promised to be happy, peaceful and contented now, free from tears and fears. And Aina valued and loved her newly formed family.

Now her mother was Bijli who had made a sacrifice and given her a better life. Thus Aina had the blessings of a wonderfully loving and caring mother.

Now, Aina had a doting father, Kalka, who came whenever he could. He had stopped drinking. He was no longer a father to loathe for his weakness for alcohol.

Now, Aina had her brother Laila, who had helped her since the baby had been born and been such a loving support. Even when Daman, Manav and Rocoo had come, Laila had been looking after Khushi inside, in another room. Aina was very proud of him.

Now Heera, her husband, was so wonderful. Heera made her feel special. She was first priority for him and his love was truly selfless, unconditional and genuine. It made her feel so precious.

Yes, it was love. She loved all of them and now all of them would live harmoniously, for ever, as a family, with a lot of giving and understanding which all of them would pass on to their lovely baby Khushi. Her Khushi!

Thus Aina's endeavour had been fulfilled as she was her own person now with a strong entity, self esteem, confidence and individuality. In her quest too, Aina had finally got the blessings of love in abundance.